"Anything else you want to practice?"

"Just this." She rose on tiptoe and brushed her lips across his mouth. She meant it to be a quick kiss. Sweet and gentle. Something to whet his appetite, give him a tantalizing taste of the woman she'd become.

Leave him wanting more.

But she hadn't counted on the warmth of his mouth, the softness of his lips or the soapy clean, all-male scent of him tickling her nostrils and sending a current of desire through her body. She couldn't be the only one feeling this electricity between them, could she?

Ivy pressed against him and flicked his lips with her tongue, willing him to open up to her. With a primal moan he surrendered, parting his lips and bringing his hands around to cup her bottom. The movement brought her impossibly closer to him, fitting her soft curves to his hard lines.

Oh. My. Bleeping. God. Seeing him in the G-string at the photo shoot hadn't prepared her for the delicious pressure of his hard body. She relaxed into the kiss, letting the sensations left in the wake of his roaming hands overwhelm her...

Dear Reader,

Friends to lovers. Brother's best friend. Ugly duckling turned swan. They're three of my favorite romance tropes, and I loved mashing them up in *Triple Dare*, the third book in my The Art of Seduction series.

Ivy Nelson has had a thing for Cade Hardesty, her twin brother Gabe's best friend, since they ate paste together in kindergarten. But he never saw her as anything more than a friend. After years traveling the world as a successful photographer, she's back in town—thirty pounds slimmer—to help run her family's business while her father recovers from a heart attack.

Sparks fly when firefighter Cade walks in to a photo session for a charity calendar and finds Ivy behind the camera. When a sexy dare forces them to spend time together, the sparks turn into a five-alarm fire. But will the flames die out when Ivy returns to her glamorous career? Or will she and Cade find a way to keep the home fires burning?

This book is special to me because it includes my absolute favorite first line (and scene) I've written to date. Let me know if you agree! I love hearing from readers. You can find me on Facebook at facebook.com/ReginaKyleauthor and on Twitter at @Regina_Kyle1. Or sign up for my newsletter at reginakyle.com and get all the news about my upcoming releases firsthand.

Up next: the youngest Nelson sibling, Noelle, gets her turn at bat. Appropriate, since it's bad boy baseball player Jace Monroe who's got her tied in knots.

Until next time,

Regina

Regina Kyle

Triple Dare

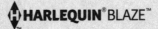

Recycling programs
for this product may
not exist in your area.

ISBN-13: 978-0-373-79877-3

Triple Dare

Copyright © 2015 by Denise Smoker

All rights reserved. Except for use in any review, the reproduction or utilization of this work in whole or in part in any form by any electronic, mechanical or other means, now known or hereinafter invented, including xerography, photocopying and recording, or in any information storage or retrieval system, is forbidden without the written permission of the publisher, Harlequin Enterprises Limited, 225 Duncan Mill Road, Don Mills, Ontario M3B 3K9, Canada.

This is a work of fiction. Names, characters, places and incidents are either the product of the author's imagination or are used fictitiously, and any resemblance to actual persons, living or dead, business establishments, events or locales is entirely coincidental.

This edition published by arrangement with Harlequin Books S.A.

For questions and comments about the quality of this book, please contact us at CustomerService@Harlequin.com.

® and TM are trademarks of Harlequin Enterprises Limited or its corporate affiliates. Trademarks indicated with ® are registered in the United States Patent and Trademark Office, the Canadian Intellectual Property Office and in other countries.

Printed in U.S.A.

www.Harlequin.com

Regina Kyle was destined to be an author when she won a story contest at age eight with a touching tale about a squirrel and a nut pie. By day, she composes dry legal briefs. At night, she writes steamy romance with heart and humor. A lover of all things theatrical, Regina lives with her husband, teenage daughter and two melodramatic cats. When she's not writing, she's usually singing, reading, cooking or watching bad reality television.

Books by Regina Kyle

Harlequin Blaze

The Art of Seduction

Triple Threat
Triple Time

To get the inside scoop on Harlequin Blaze and its talented writers, be sure to check out BlazeAuthors.com.

All backlist available in ebook format.

Visit the author profile page at Harlequin.com for more titles.

This one's for my peeps at CTRWA, especially my critique partner, Lisa Hayden, without whom my books would probably be all dialogue and no deep POV; my Obi-Wan, Jane Haertel; the plot vixens, Gail Chianese, Jamie Pope, Jamie Beck and our fearless leader, Heidi Ulrich; my sweet and sassy signing sister, Katy Lee; and my conference roomies, Melanie Meadors and Jen Moncuse. These intrepid ladies have cheered my successes and held my hand through the rough patches (or smacked me upside the head, if needed). They put up with my idiosyncrasies, my moodiness and, in some cases, my snoring. There is absolutely no doubt in my mind that I wouldn't be in the position to write this dedication without them. I am eternally grateful for their support and, more importantly, their friendship.

1

"CADE ALEXANDER HARDESTY! Get your half-naked ass out here before I come back there and strip you myself!"

Cade stared at the outfit in his hands. If you could call a red satin G-string an outfit. Did Ivy seriously expect him to wear this? He figured she'd photograph him in his turnout gear, maybe shirtless with his bunker pants unbuttoned and riding low on his hips. After all, the "Hunks of Burning Love" calendar was an annual institution, featuring Stockton's finest firefighters in various states of undress, each year for a different charity. This time it was the local animal shelter, a cause he supported 100 percent.

But a G-string? What the hell did she think he was, a Chippendales dancer?

"I'll be way more than half-naked in this thing." He dangled the undersized jockstrap from a finger and held it over the top of the changing screen.

"I'm not kidding, Mr. December. I haven't got all day. Put it on and get out here."

Cade groaned and kicked off his sneakers.

"You've got to the count of three. One…"

He stripped off his T-shirt. "Two…"

His pants and boxer briefs hit the floor.

"Three."

Cade stepped gingerly into the G-string. *Shit.* The ridiculous scrap of fabric barely hid anything. He tried adjusting himself without much success.

"Uh, Ivy? We have a problem."

"Damn straight we do. I distinctly heard myself say 'three' and you're still hiding back there like a whore at a church social."

Cade chuckled in spite of his predicament. Ivy had always been able to make him laugh. They'd done lots of crazy things together as kids—him, Ivy and his best friend, her twin brother, Gabe. Sticking crayons up their noses in kindergarten. Smoking behind the high school gym. Stealing their football rival's mascot, an uncooperative goat they tried—and failed—to hide in the Nelsons' treehouse.

Okay, so the last two had pretty much been him and Ivy. She was fearless, willing to take any dare they threw at her if it meant she could tag along. Hell, she'd even seen him naked. Of course, they'd been six at the time and running through the sprinkler in her backyard.

"All right, big guy. Ready or not, here I come."

"I'm ready, I'm ready."

Cade took a deep breath, reminding himself for the hundredth time that this whole thing was for charity, and stepped out from behind the screen.

"Hang on. I almost forgot." He caught a glimpse of Ivy's apple bottom as she darted into the tiny office in the corner of the studio. She'd been in there when he arrived, too, yelling out instructions for him to change and wait for her.

He frowned, surveying the room. Wood floor, bare walls, white backdrop, a few umbrella lights. Her camera sat on a tripod in the middle of it all, ready for action. What else could she need? "Forgot what?"

"The final touches to your costume."

"You mean there's more to this getup than dental floss?"

"Not exactly." She emerged from the office with a Santa hat in one hand and a gray-and-white calico kitten in the other, cradled against her chest. But it wasn't the cat or the hat that had Cade's attention. It was Ivy.

Holy three-alarm fire.

It'd been twelve years since she'd left Stockton. And almost three since he'd seen her on one of her rare visits home.

Those years had treated her well.

"What are you wearing?" His heart rate kicked up a notch as he took in the short shorts and tight V-necked T-shirt that clung to her lush curves. I Like To Flash People was emblazoned across her breasts. Where the hell were the usual baggy jeans and oversized sweatshirt? Even her hair was different, the normally wild, auburn curls restrained in some sort of messy bun that women seemed to think was sexy. He'd been inclined to disagree, until now.

"A damn sight more than you." She handed him the kitten and put the hat on his head, adjusting it so it sat at an angle, away from his eyes.

"Don't blame me. You're the one who picked this thing." He plucked at the waistband of his skimpy G-string with his free hand. The kitten squirmed in the other, its soft fur tickling Cade's palm. He rested it against his shoulder and it burrowed under his chin.

"Actually, it was Hank." Her brows knitted at the mention of the photographer who'd done the calendar for as long as anyone could remember. He'd thrown his back out, and thankfully Ivy had been in town to step in. "I'm just finishing what he started."

"None of the other guys had to dress like strippers."

"None of the other guys has a body like yours." She turned to fiddle with her camera but not before he caught her eyeing his package. Interesting. She'd always thought of him like a brother. Hadn't she? There was that one time senior year…

"I heard they've been trying to get you to pose for years," she continued, interrupting his thoughts. "What finally made you do it?"

He shrugged and stepped in front of the backdrop, where he assumed she wanted him. "My mom wasn't comfortable with the garden club seeing her little boy in the buff. But she and Dad retired to Chapel Hill last year, so…"

Ivy chuckled. "What they don't know won't hurt them?"

"Something like that. And if they find out, at least they're a thousand miles away." Although, knowing his mother, she'd find some way to punish him long-distance.

Ivy peered through the camera lens, focusing on who knew what, then straightened, hands on her hips. The movement thrust her already prominent breasts out even farther. *Hot damn.* Had she always been so…well-endowed? Is that what she'd been hiding under all the loose-fitting clothes?

Whoa, slugger. Don't go there. She's practically your sister. Of course, there's a big difference between practically *and* actually.

"Well." She let out a puff of air, ruffling the loose tendrils of hair that had escaped her bun. "Let's get this show on the road, then."

Cade stroked the kitten with his index finger. "Where do you want us?"

She waved a hand. "You're fine right there for the moment. I have to aim the lights."

He shifted from one foot to the other, petting the cat and trying not to stare at the junk in her trunk while she fine-tuned first one light, then another. "What's the cat's name?" he asked to break the silence.

"Bilbo."

"Someone's a Tolkien fan."

"The warden." Her Chuck Taylors—the lone hold-over from her teenage wardrobe—squeaked on the varnished floor as she moved on to the third light. "He's up for adoption."

"The warden?" Cade asked, smirking.

"Bilbo, obviously." Ivy stopped tinkering with the light long enough to shoot him a pleading look over her shoulder.

"No, thanks. I'm more of a dog person. Couldn't the shelter have set me up with a rottweiler? Or even a shih tzu?"

"Nothing sells calendars like a big, strong guy cuddling a cute, little kitten." She finished with the last light and walked back to the tripod. "Besides, the chief got the rottweiler. And they didn't have a shih tzu."

"So you think I'm big and strong?" He couldn't resist teasing her and flexed his biceps.

"Please." She rolled her eyes. "You've got the entire female population of Stockton to stroke your ego. You don't need me."

He corralled Bilbo, who had climbed over his shoulder and perched on the back of his neck. "You mean Maude at the diner, who celebrated her eighty-fifth birthday last week? Or the librarian, Mrs. Frazier? She can whistle 'Bohemian Rhapsody' through her dentures."

"Gabe says you're dating the new checkout girl at Gibson's Grocery with the amazing—"

"Smile?" He waggled an eyebrow. "Hair? Ability to add four-digit numbers in her head?"

"Yeah, right." She crossed to a table against the far wall. "Put Bilbo down for a second. And stand with your feet apart, arms out."

He lowered the kitten to the floor and crossed his arms in front of his chest. "Why would I do that?"

She turned, a translucent spray bottle filled with colorless liquid in her hand, and sauntered toward him, looking like a lioness bearing down on her prey. Was that some kind of oil? She wasn't going to…

"Duh. Why else? So I can wet you down. Now shut up and spread 'em."

Damn.

Ivy Nelson tried to maintain an air of cool, disinterested professionalism as she strode forward, holding the spray bottle of water and glycerin in front of her like a deadly weapon. But it wasn't easy. Cade Hardesty in all his nearly naked glory was even hotter than she'd imagined. And she'd done a heck of a lot of imagining.

She slowed then stopped, her legs turned to wax. The hand with the bottle dropped to her side and she swallowed hard. With her free hand, she tugged on the hem of her shirt, suddenly aware of the wide expanse of fleshy, chalk-white skin showing above the waist-band of her shorts.

Stop it. So what if you're not a size two—or even an eight? You're not Jabba the Mutt anymore.

She tightened her grip on the bottle, squeezing it so hard the plastic crinkled in her fist, and steeled her resolve. She'd photographed hundreds of models, male and female. Had her hands all over some of the best bodies in the business. Cade was no different.

Except he was. He was her first love, the boy she'd spent her youth doodling about in her notebook even though he'd never seen her as more than his best friend's pesky twin sister, an easy mark for a dare and good for an occasional laugh.

"Are we going to do this or what?" The boy was a man now, the picture of masculine yumminess with his arms crossed over his broad, tanned chest, all hard lines and warm, firm muscle. Years of high school and college athletics followed by a career fighting fires had honed his body into sheer male perfection. Bulging biceps. Washboard abs. Powerful thighs and toned, trim calves. Hell, even his bare feet were sexy. And as for what the G-string was so not hiding…

The hairs rose on Ivy's arms and the back of her neck. *Hell to the yes. We're going to do this, all right.*

"Earth to Ivy." Cade brushed a lock of honey-blond hair from his forehead, revealing baby blues framed by impossibly long lashes, perfect for a woman, downright sinful on a man. "I'm freezing my ass off here."

She craned her neck to risk a glance at his backside. Nope. His fine, firm ass was most definitely still there.

"I'll turn down the AC." Her false bravado back in

place, she sashayed past him and raised the thermostat until she heard it click off.

Great. She was already burning up. Now she just might burst into flames.

Why did Hank have to hurt his back? And why had she agreed to fill in for him? She hadn't even been home a week. She was supposed to be taking care of her dad after his heart attack, not ogling scantily clad firefighters. Especially ones she'd known since grade school.

Well, she'd be done after this shoot. Then she'd spend the rest of her time in Stockton working in her parents' greenhouse and making sure her dad took his meds and followed a low-cholesterol diet. No time for lusting after her childhood BFF. And slim to no chance of running into him, or anyone else from the so-called glory days of high school. Days she'd just as soon forget.

"Better?" Ivy faced her subject, who had Bilbo in his arms again. The cat's loud purrs echoed in the almost empty room as Cade rubbed slow circles on his belly.

Oh, yeah. They'd definitely saved the best for last.

"Sorry." Cade gave her a sheepish grin and her heart flip-flopped. "The little guy was lonely."

"Sure you don't want to take him home?"

"No can do. Like I said, dog person."

She eyed the kitten, sprawled belly-up across Cade's folded arms, the picture of feline ecstasy with his head back and eyes closed. "Bilbo seems to disagree."

"He'll get snapped up in no time. Probably by some nice family with kids who'll smother him with affection."

Cade had a point. Puppies and kittens practically flew out of the shelter. It was the full-grown dogs and cats that had a hard time finding a home. She'd adopt one herself if she wasn't on the road all the time. But Cade…

"How about an older pet? The shelter has lots of them, and they're harder to place."

"Maybe someday. Right now I'm too busy with work and…stuff."

"Stuff like the checkout girl at Gibson's?" She wanted to swallow the words as soon as they left her mouth. What right did she have to be jealous? Cade was single, barely thirty and way more than reasonably attractive. He could date anyone he wanted.

Too bad he didn't want her. Oh, well. *Qué será, será*, lots more fish in the sea and all that crap.

"What is this, a photo shoot or the Spanish Inquisition?" His slow smile took any sting there might have been out of his words. "And I thought Gabe was the king of cross-examination."

"Please." She walked back to the tripod and patted her Nikon D3. "He may be an attorney, but I can expose as much through this lens as he can in court."

"So how about we get started?" He nodded to the bottle still in her hand. "You gonna use that thing or not?"

She stepped back and studied him as impartially as she could, taking off her love-struck schoolgirl glasses and donning her seasoned, award-winning photographer hat. She bit her lip, nodding as she noted the way the light reflected off his well-developed pecs, the dusting of golden hair leading to his navel, the shadowy vee where his hips met his thighs.

"Not." She set the bottle on the floor, plucked the camera off the tripod and pocketed the lens cap. Cade was a full-fledged, red-blooded, all-American male. Every woman's dream. He didn't need phony enhancements or photographer's gimmicks to make him look good. This shoot called for something different. Something daring.

Something…real.

"Turn around."

"What?"

"You heard me. Turn around. And put Bilbo on your shoulder."

He faced the backdrop and draped the cat over his left shoulder. "Trying to get my best side?"

"Something like that." She hit the power button on the Nikon and peered through the lens. "Good. Now look at Bilbo."

Cade turned his head and stared awkwardly at the cat.

"Relax." Ivy lowered the camera. "Pet him. Talk to him."

He scratched the cat between the ears. "What do you want me to say?"

"Anything." She brought the camera back up to her face, determined to focus on the interaction between man and beast and not Cade's buns of steel in that obscene thong. "Tell him how cute he is. Regale him with the details of your latest conquest. Recite *Green Eggs and Ham*. Just have fun with it."

"Did you hear that, little guy?" He stroked down the cat's back, pulling lightly on his tail. "We're supposed to be having fun."

Bilbo's loud purrs increased, and his pink tongue stole out to lick Cade's sexily stubbled chin. Cade threw back his head and laughed, flashing a million-watt smile that transformed his already handsome face into a thing of beauty.

"Oh, my God, that's perfect." Ivy snapped away as

she moved around him, trying to capture every possible angle. "Don't stop. That look will have these calendars sailing off the shelves."

For the next hour, she posed him. Standing. Sitting. Reclining on a dusty settee they dragged out of the office and brushed off. Of course, that meant she had to feel that hot, hard flesh scorching her palm every time she adjusted an arm or repositioned a leg.

All in a day's work.

Right. Then why hadn't any of the professionals she'd photographed over the years—men as muscular and manly as Cade—made her heart flutter, her breath catch and her fingers tingle with the need to do more than touch?

Fortunately—or unfortunately—she'd had to do less and less touching as the shoot went on and Cade loosened up. He was a natural, better than some of the models she'd worked with. And Bilbo was a regular feline ham, mugging it up like he was born to be in front of the camera.

They were quite the pair. Women would go gaga over them.

Over him.

Ivy snapped the lens cap on the camera with more force than necessary, trying to ignore the ugly pang of resentment that started in her stomach and yanked at her heart.

"Okay." She returned the camera to the tripod and reached for the cat. "I think we've got what we need. And Bilbo has to get back to the shelter before closing time."

"I can bring him." Cade stood, his hold tightening on the wriggling kitten. "It's on my way."

"Your way to what?" She swiped a stray, sweat-dampened hair off her cheek and went to lower the thermostat. "The firehouse is in the opposite direction."

"I'm not on duty tonight. I've got a date."

"Your Gibson's girl with the banging…math skills?"

He whipped off the Santa hat and pressed it to his chest in mock horror. "A gentleman never kisses and tells."

"Since when are you a gentleman?" She took the cat from him and pushed him toward the changing screen in the corner. "Go get dressed. I'll put Bilbo in his carrier so you can drop him off and be on time for your hot date."

And she could get back to her dad and the nursery and quit fantasizing about God's gift to womankind.

As if.

2

"SHE'S BEAUTIFUL, HOLS." Ivy looked down at her infant niece and brushed a knuckle over one alabaster cheek. "A perfect little angel."

"Sure, now that she's sleeping." Holly sank into the Adirondack chair next to Ivy's, stretched out her legs and ran her toes through the grass. "How is it I rock her for hours without success yet you hold her for two seconds and she's out like a light?"

Ivy frowned at the dark circles under her sister's eyes. Anyone else in Holly's position—Broadway playwright, married to a movie star—would have hired someone to plan her daughter's christening. Turned it into a media event. But not Holly. She'd insisted on doing everything herself and keeping it small, just family and a few close friends.

"Auntie's magic touch, I guess." Ivy tucked the lemon-yellow fleece blanket under her niece's tiny chin. It might be spring, but evenings were cool in Connecticut, even with a blaze roaring in the fire pit.

"Too bad you're not around more. I could use a bit of that magic every now and then."

Holly's husband, Nick, came up behind her and dropped a kiss on her upturned forehead. "How's that for magic?"

"It's a start." Holly pulled him back down to her and kissed him soundly.

Ivy's heartstrings tugged as she watched them, immersed in each other, clearly ass-over-teakettle in love. Not that she begrudged Holly her happiness. Her sister deserved it after everything her sleazeball ex-husband put her through. But part of Ivy—the part that wondered how much longer she could go on globe-trotting—couldn't help wanting a little of that happiness for herself.

She hid her melancholy with a lukewarm chuckle. "Would you two get a room already?"

Nick came up for air and waved an arm at the rambling clapboard house across the lawn. "We've got ten of them. We just have to get rid of our guests."

"How about we get Joy in her crib first? She's had a long day, and it's awfully chilly out here."

Holly started to stand but Nick stopped her with a hand on her shoulder. "Relax. I've got her. You've done enough today."

"I still can't believe you kept Dad's name thing going," Ivy said, shaking her head at her sister. Their father loved Christmas and had played Santa in the local holiday parade for as long as anyone could remember. He'd given his children names reminiscent of the season: Holly, Ivy, Gabriel and Noelle. It had been a constant source of embarrassment as kids. And now Holly and Nick had followed suit with Joy.

"Did we really have a choice?" Holly exchanged a

knowing look with her husband. "I mean, I married a guy with the same name as St. Nicholas."

"And Joy was born on Christmas Eve." Nick took the sleeping baby from Ivy's arms. Joy stirred briefly, then settled into her father's embrace.

"Why not Eve, then?"

"Too obvious. We were going for something more subtle." Holly swiveled her head to watch Nick as he strode up the lawn toward the house. "Send Devin down," she called after him. "And tell her to bring the stuff for the s'mores. It's on the counter next to the stove."

"Sure thing." He disappeared into the increasing darkness.

"Too bad Noelle couldn't stay for dessert." Ivy stared across the grass to the dock jutting out over Leffert's Pond. A rowboat bobbed at the end, partially obscuring the moon's reflection in the calm, glasslike water. For the second time in as many minutes, she felt a twinge of envy toward her sister. Great guy. Great kid. Great house.

"I know," Holly agreed. "She had to get back to the city for an early rehearsal tomorrow."

"Mom finally get Dad out the door?"

"Yeah. I'm surprised he held out as long as he did. We offered to postpone the christening, but he wouldn't hear of it. Stubborn Swede." Holly gave a halfhearted shrug and tipped her head skyward.

"Oh, I almost forgot. Cade should be here any minute."

Ivy barely stopped herself from bolting upright. She hadn't seen Cade since he'd walked out of her studio two weeks ago. She continued to gaze out at the lake, her face an impassive mask. She hoped. "I thought you said he was on call."

"Only until seven o'clock. That's why he missed the ceremony. But he promised to stop by when he got off."

Ivy closed her eyes against the image of Cade "getting off." In the shower, head thrown back, one arm braced against the tile as he stroked himself to completion. In her bed, over her, under her, in her, until they both collapsed, exhausted but satisfied.

Damn. She thought she had it bad before. Seeing him nearly naked had sent her off the high dive into an ocean of lust.

"Are you okay? You look flushed."

"I'm fine." Ivy put a hand to her face. Red-hot. "A little too close to the fire, I guess." She fanned herself. Like that was going to douse the inferno raging inside her.

"Rumor has it you got to see him in his birthday suit." Holly leaned forward. "Is he as scrumptious as I think he is?"

"First off, he was not 'in his birthday suit.'" Ivy put air quotes around the last four words. "He was wearing a thong."

"That much, huh?" Holly snickered.

Ivy ignored her and played with the zipper on her hoodie. "Second, it was all business."

"Some business."

"And third, you're married to *People*'s sexiest man alive. What do you care how Cade or any other guy looks naked?"

"Married. Not dead. I can still appreciate a fine male form." Holly leaned in farther, resting her elbows on her knees. "So come on. Spill. How fine is he?"

Ivy let out a slow, resigned sigh. She hadn't won an

argument with her big sister in years, and it didn't look like today would be any different. "Let's just say December's going to be a whole heck of a lot hotter next year."

"December? That's like a year and a half from now. Can't you give me a sneak peek?"

"Nope. Photographers' code of ethics."

"There's a photographers' code of ethics?"

"Well, there should be." Ivy tucked her knees to her chest.

"Fine. Be that way." Holly settled back into her chair. "I suppose I can't complain. I mean, you're taking care of Dad. And the nursery. You know I'd stay and help, but…"

"It's okay. You've got enough going on with the baby and your new show in rehearsals. It's my turn to pitch in. Besides—" Ivy scanned the newly reconstructed dock, impeccably landscaped yard and sprawling house "—you're letting me stay here. That's not exactly a hardship. Especially when the alternative was staying with Mom and Dad."

"They driving you nuts?"

Ivy could hear the smile in her sister's voice. She smiled back. "Not yet. But close."

"I just wish it hadn't taken a heart attack to bring you home." Holly reached out to cover Ivy's hand on the faded wooden armrest. "I missed you."

"Ditto." A lump of guilt clogged Ivy's throat. She'd fled Stockton, so desperate to reinvent herself she'd run from anything that reminded her of the girl she'd been. But in doing so she'd alienated herself from her family, too.

A mistake she needed to rectify. And maybe helping out her parents was a good start.

"This where the party's at?" Devin's voice drifted down from the house.

Ivy turned and saw her ambling toward them, a tray balanced on one hand. Gabe walked beside her and a third, shadowy figure lagged a few paces behind them.

"Look what the cat dragged in." Gabe gestured at the silhouette, whose features became more distinct with each step.

"Got room for one more?" Cade held up two six-packs of chocolate stout. "I brought suds."

CADE TOOK A pull on his bottle of stout and leaned back in the weathered wooden chair, one of eight surrounding the fire pit. Holly had gone up to the house to see if her husband needed help with the baby, and Devin had followed a few minutes later, pleading exhaustion.

Leaving the Three Amigos to relive their glory days.

Sort of.

"That is so not what happened." Ivy fixed her brother with a defiant stare.

"Is too," Gabe countered. "I distinctly remember you falling into the pool in the middle of the boys' swim team practice."

"You're delusional." She shook her head, making her reddish brown curls, free from the bun she'd worn the last time he'd seen her, sway and shimmer in the firelight.

Cade stared into the flames, fighting the squeezing sensation in his gut. This—this feeling—was why he'd almost thrown Holly's invitation into the circular file. But whatever issues he had with his mother, she'd raised him better than that. The Nelsons were like family to him, even more than his egg and sperm donors. They'd given him what his parents couldn't—affection. Warmth. A sense of belonging.

And you didn't skip out on family, no matter how hard it was for him to be near Ivy without getting turned on.

"Am not." Gabe swigged his beer.

"Are too. Right Cade?" Even in the half glow of the fire, Cade could feel Ivy's hazel eyes piercing him. "You were there."

"Oh, no." He waved a palm at her. "Leave me out. I'm not getting in the middle of this."

"Traitor. I wouldn't have been there in the first place if you hadn't dared me to fill the pool with rubber ducks."

Cade smiled at the memory. "You never could resist a dare. But you didn't get the pool filled, did you?"

"Yeah." Gabe chuckled. "Because she fell in."

"I never said I didn't fall in." Ivy stuck out her chin defiantly. "Just not during swim team practice."

"You know what that means?" Cade ran a finger around the rim of his beer bottle.

"Not a clue." She pulled her sweatshirt tighter around her, emphasizing those full, firm breasts he hadn't been able to stop thinking about since the photo shoot. "But I'm sure you're planning to enlighten me."

He shifted in his seat to hide the evidence of his reaction to her. "You owe me. One dare."

Gabe's chuckle turned into a guffaw.

"Oh, please." Ivy turned to Cade, swinging that damn curtain of hair and sending another jolt of tension through his midsection. "That was more than ten years ago. You can't be serious."

"As ammonium nitrate."

"I don't even know what that is."

"Come on, Ivy." He had no idea why, but he felt an

instant, overwhelming desire for her to agree, as though some stupid dare would bring them closer together again. And why did he care about that anyway? She'd be out of town faster than a flashover as soon as her dad was on his feet again. It would be safer for both of them if he just kept his distance. So why couldn't he? "For old times' sake."

"No way. I'm not a kid anymore. I'm a professional, with a reputation to uphold."

"I promise it won't be anything illegal."

"Yeah, right." She dragged the toe of her sneaker through the grass.

"Or harmful."

"Says the guy who made me drink an entire jar of pickle juice." Ivy grimaced. "And then eat all the salt at the bottom of the pretzel bag."

Yeah, Cade remembered that one. She'd puked her guts out. For hours. He'd felt terrible about it, not that he'd let her know. "Give me a break. I was thirteen."

"Which only means you've had seventeen years since then to come up with something even more diabolical."

Any snarky response Cade could have come up with was preempted by his cell phone ringing. He pulled it out of his pants pocket, knowing—and dreading—what was coming.

"Shit." He pressed Reject, turned the damn thing off and stowed it back in his pocket.

"What's wrong?" Gabe crossed to a pile of wood on the opposite side of the fire pit, picked up a log and tossed it into the flames, making sparks fly into the cool night air. "Your mother after you again?"

"Nah." Cade glanced at Ivy, wishing he didn't have to air his dirty laundry in front of her. He drained his beer, then opened the cooler next to his chair, dropped in the empty and pulled out a fresh bottle. "Sasha. She keeps texting and calling. Even showed up at the station this afternoon bearing brownies."

He grabbed another beer from the cooler and held it out to Gabe.

Gabe took it and returned to his seat. "The guys must've loved that."

Yeah. They'd never let Cade live it down. They were already calling him Brownie Boy.

"Can I have one of those?" Ivy pointed to the cooler. "And who's Sasha?"

"Cade's girlfriend."

"Ex-girlfriend," Cade amended, opening a bottle and handing it to her. Their fingers brushed and he felt a flicker of something electric pass between them. "As of two weeks ago."

His date with Sasha the night of the photo shoot had been their last. Not that the session had anything to do with their breakup. It was pure coincidence he'd picked that night to call it quits.

Wasn't it?

"Do I know her?" Ivy wrinkled her nose. "I don't remember a Sasha from high school."

"She's a few years younger than us."

"That's an understatement." Gabe snorted. "She's barely legal."

"She's twenty-one," Cade said through clenched teeth. "Almost twenty-two."

"Let me guess." Ivy swung her legs sideways over one arm of her chair and took a slug of beer. "The checkout girl with the—"

"Never mind." Cade cut her off with a glare. "That's

not important. What is important is no matter what I say, she won't leave me alone."

"There's your problem." Gabe, always the analytical one, rubbed his chin thoughtfully. "You know the old saying about actions speaking louder than words."

"Sure." Cade popped the top of his beer and took a long, slow sip. "But what's that got to do with Sasha?"

Gabe crossed one Sperry-clad foot over his knee. "You need to show her you mean business, not just tell her."

"Show her how?"

"By dating someone else."

"Like who?"

"I don't know." Gabe lifted a shoulder. "You're the local ladies' man. You tell me."

"Yeah, well, that's the problem." Cade picked at the label on his beer bottle. "Stockton's not all that big. I've sort of exhausted the dating pool."

"Hello." Ivy waggled her fingers at him. "Available female here."

"Huh?" Cade couldn't have heard her right. She did not just offer herself up to him like a virgin sacrifice.

"I volunteer as tribute."

She did.

He continued to stare at her, not sure how to respond. Gabe, on the other hand, had no such problem. He burst into hysterical laughter.

"What's so funny?" Ivy pressed her lips into a thin line.

"You?" Gabe choked out between laughs. "And Cade? You might as well be brother and sister."

Only Cade didn't think of her that way, not anymore. And that was exactly why he didn't want to go out with her. Couldn't go out with her.

"Look, Ivy, I appreciate the offer but…"

"But what?" She crossed and uncrossed her legs over the arm of the chair, giving him a tantalizing glimpse of creamy flesh under the hem of her shorts. "Are you chicken? Afraid you'll succumb to my many charms?"

"Not exactly." *Liar.*

"Hang on." Gabe grinned over the lip of his beer bottle, his laughter finally contained. "The more I think about it, it's actually pretty perfect. You don't have to really go out. Just show up somewhere Sasha will be and pretend you're a couple. That should be enough to get her to back off."

Great. Pretend dating. Being together and not at the same time. "I don't know…"

"Come on, man." Gabe's grin widened. "What have you got to lose?"

His mind. His heart. The only family he'd ever known if things got serious and then they crashed and burned.

"Tell you what." Ivy's tone softened. "Consider it my way of satisfying the dare."

"Since when does the dare-*ee* get to decide her own terms?"

"Since the dar-*er* needs her help to get rid of his ex."

"Okay." The corners of his mouth curled upward as he thought of a way to play along without risking anything. "One date. You can come watch me tear it up at third base in the Battle of the Badges game."

"Battle of the Badges?"

"Softball—cops versus firefighters. They kicked our asses last year." Cade tipped back his beer, letting the rich, chocolatey liquid slide down his throat, and mentally patted himself on the back. It was genius. Him on the field. Ivy in the stands, cheering him on. Sasha watching the whole thing. He'd convince his ex it was over and still keep Ivy at a safe distance.

"One tiny flaw in your plan." Ivy shifted her legs back over the arm of the chair and sat facing forward. "How do you know Sasha will be there?"

"Oh, she'll be there," Gabe chimed in. "It's a huge event. Almost the whole town turns out. Winners get bragging rights and pizza after the game, courtesy of the losers."

"How come I've never been? Never even heard of it." Ivy's nose wrinkled again. A habit of hers, apparently.

Cade frowned, wondering why he'd never noticed it before. What else had he missed? He shook off the thought and focused on answering Ivy's question. "We only started playing a few years ago."

"When is it?"

"Friday at six."

"All I'd have to do is watch you play?" Ivy bit her lip. The unconsciously erotic gesture sent his sex drive into orbit.

Cade cleared his throat and scraped a hand through his hair. "And root for me. Maybe wear my extra jersey. Typical girlfriend stuff."

A strange look crossed her face, and for a moment he thought she was going to say no. But then she stood, chugged the rest of her beer and faced him.

"Okay. Pick me up at five thirty. And don't forget the jersey."

3

IVY CURSED HERSELF for the thousandth time as she pulled back the curtain and peered out the upstairs window, watching for Cade's SUV. What the hell had she been thinking? Or maybe she hadn't been. One too many chocolate stouts and her damned ego had gotten her into this mess.

But she couldn't help it. It had hurt like hell when Gabe and Cade started discussing the eligible female population of Stockton as if she wasn't sitting two feet away. What, pray tell, was wrong with her? Did they think she wasn't good enough for Cade, that no one would believe a super stud like him would date a girl like her?

She wasn't Jabba the Mutt anymore. She wasn't.

Not that those two dumb-asses recognized it. To them she'd always be an overweight, insecure, pimply-faced kid.

Well, she'd show them. Especially the chief dumb-ass. Cade.

Ivy abandoned her vigil at the window and headed for the full-length mirror in the master bathroom, needing one last confirmation that all her primping had paid off. Hair tamed in a ponytail, adorably pulled through the back of a Stockton Fire Department baseball cap she'd found in Holly's closet? Check. Just enough makeup to hide her freckles and play up the pale green flecks in her hazel eyes? Check. Legs tanned, shaved and showcased in an appropriately snug pair of denim cutoffs? Check.

She smiled at her reflection, thinking back to a few years ago when *tight* had been a four-letter word in her fashion vocabulary. If there was one thing Andre had taught her—over and above all the lessons in photography she'd learned as his apprentice-turned-associate—it was that she wasn't doing herself any favors wearing clothes that looked like they were designed by Omar the tent maker. "Remember," he'd said. "You wear the clothes. They don't wear you."

Well, she'd wear the hell out of this outfit. She grabbed a pair of silver hoop earrings and her collection of Alex and Ani bracelets off the counter and started downstairs, humming the latest pop radio earworm courtesy of Taylor Swift. All she needed now was Cade's jersey, which he'd promised to bring. She'd look a little strange if she showed up in only a sports bra. Even if it did wonders for her double Ds.

The doorbell rang when she was halfway down.

"Be right there," she called, taking the rest of the steps two at a time.

But when she got to the door, her hand on the knob, she froze.

You got this, girl. Show him little Ivy Nelson's all grown up.

Her heart pounding and her palms moist, she swung open the door. "Hi. Come on in. I'm almost ready."

She stood back to let him pass, but he stayed firmly planted on the stoop with a dazed expression on his face. "I, uh, brought this."

He thrust out one hand, a fire-engine-red jersey clenched in his fist. He wore an identical one, the initials SFD across his chest, tucked into a pair of form-fitting, gray baseball pants.

"Thanks," she said, the tremble almost gone from her voice. Amazing what a little good, old-fashioned leering could do for a girl's self-confidence. She pried the shirt from his fingers, tossed it onto her shoulder and motioned him inside. "I'll go put it on and we can get out of here. Can't have you missing batting practice."

He followed her in. "We don't have batting practice, but I should probably stretch before game time."

"I can help." She stood in front of the half mirror in the foyer and slipped on her jewelry. "A model taught me some great partner exercises on set in the Turks and Caicos."

She didn't mention that the model worked for Victoria's Secret and that the shoot was for their swimsuit edition. No need to conjure up comparisons between her size-ten frame and the ideal 34-25-34 figure of a VS girl.

"Sounds good." He leaned against the doorjamb. "Sasha ought to get the picture pretty quick if she sees us working out together."

Right. How could she forget? This was all for show. For Sasha. Not real. Not for her.

Ivy unbuttoned the jersey and slipped it on, determined not to let Cade's comment burst the bubble of self-assurance she was floating in thanks to his initial reaction. She had him for tonight, and she was going to make the most of it.

The shirt hung well past her hips, like she thought it would. A throwback to her Jabba days. But she had a plan for that. She pulled the ends together and tied them securely at her waist, checking in the mirror to make sure it had the anticipated effect of highlighting her breasts while revealing just enough—but not too much—skin.

Perfect.

"All set," she said, turning to face him.

"Damn." He eyed her up and down, his baby blues leaving goose bumps in their wake. "My shirt never looked so good."

She eyed him right back, lingering a little longer than necessary between his legs, where the baseball pants weren't hiding anything.

Down, girl.

"I don't know." She licked her lips. "It looks pretty fine on you, too."

"Oh, yeah?" He pushed off the doorjamb and took a step toward her.

"Mmm-hmm." She followed his lead, moving into him. "I've always been a sucker for a man in uniform."

He cocked his head. "Are you flirting with me?"

"Maybe." Another step and she was close enough to put a hand on his chest, praying the whole time he wouldn't brush it off. When he didn't, she let her fingers curl into the soft fabric of his jersey. His heartbeat pulsed under her palm, almost as fast as hers. "Or maybe just practicing my witty banter. You know. For Sasha."

His crystal-blue eyes darkened to indigo. "Anything else you want to practice?"

"Just this."

She rose on tiptoes and brushed her lips across his

mouth. She meant it to be a quick kiss. Sweet and gentle, something to whet his appetite and give him a tantalizing taste of the woman she'd become.

Something to leave him wanting more.

But the second her lips found his all thoughts of kissing and running flew out of her mind. She hadn't counted on the warmth of his mouth, the softness of his lips or the soapy clean, all-male scent of him tickling her nostrils and sending a current of desire through her body.

She snaked her hand around his neck and pulled his head down, needing more. Needing him to respond. She couldn't be the only one feeling this electricity between them, could she?

Ivy pressed against him and flicked her tongue against his mouth, willing him to open up to her. With a primal moan he surrendered, parting his lips and bringing his hands around to cup her bottom. The movement brought her impossibly closer to him, fitting her soft curves to his hard lines.

Oh. My. Bleeping. God. Seeing him in the G-string hadn't prepared her for the delicious pressure of his growing erection against her. She closed her eyes and relaxed into the kiss, letting the sensations left in the wake of his roaming hands overwhelm her.

He released her and stepped back, leaving her breathless and shaky. The sudden rush of air smacked her like a wet towel. She tightened her ponytail and summoned her inner Scarlett O'Hara.

"I think that ought to convince her. Don't you?"

Cade shoved his hands in his pockets. "It was pretty damn persuasive. But I doubt we'll have to go that far. Just seeing us together should do the trick."

"You never know. Better safe than sorry." Ivy grabbed

her purse from the hall table and brushed past Cade on her way to the door. Pinpricks of heat flared where they touched. She shook them off, opened the door and stepped into the mild, sweet-smelling spring evening. "Let's go. It's almost game time. We've got a grand entrance to make. And a mission to accomplish."

Cade didn't need to know Ivy's mission had a dual purpose. First, show Sasha he was off the market. And second, get him to take her seriously.

Which one would be more difficult was a toss-up.

"Strike three."

Cade threw down his batter's helmet and stalked back to the dugout.

"Here." He thrust his bat into the waiting hands of the left fielder, some guy in C Company he barely knew. "Maybe you'll have better luck with it."

"What's eating you, Hardesty?" O'Brien, the first baseman and one of Cade's fellow firefighters in B Company, greeted him with a smirk and a slap on the back. "One more at bat like that and Cappy's gonna bump you out of the cleanup spot."

"No one's taking Cade off cleanup." Like Teddy Roosevelt, George "Cappy" Perez, B Company's captain and the team manager, spoke softly and carried a big-ass stick. Right now that stick was a Louisville Slugger he leaned on in the corner of the dugout.

"It's okay, Cade, you'll get 'em next time." Ivy's cheerful voice rang across the field.

"That's right, baby." Sasha's followed, a slow, sweet twang that oozed sex. It used to turn him on. Now it was ˙ flat-out embarrassing, like she was trying too hard ˙ˑ˙ctive. "Next time."

"Now I see your problem." O'Brien leaned back on the bench and folded his beefy arms over his chest. "You've got one too many women, Hardesty. Want me to take one off your hands? I bet the redhead won't mind. Fat chicks usually aren't picky."

Cade ripped off his batting gloves, grabbed the front of O'Brien's jersey and pulled him to his feet until they were standing face-to-face. Cade could see the pores on his pug nose, crooked from being broken one too many times. "Listen up, dirtbag. If I ever hear you say another word about Ivy, I'll hit you so hard not even Google will be able to find you."

"Okay, okay. I get it." Cade pushed him away and O'Brien landed hard on the bench. "The fat chick's yours. I'll take the blonde with the big boobs."

Cade lunged for him again, but a strong arm wrapped around him from behind and held him back.

"That's enough." Cappy loosened his hold only slightly and turned his attention to Cade's antagonist. "O'Brien. Less trash talk. More softball. You're on deck. Let's get something started. I'm not buying these pansies pizza two years in a row."

O'Brien scooped up his helmet and headed for the on-deck circle, pushing past Cade and muttering something under his breath that sounded suspiciously like "chubby chaser." Cappy let go of Cade, giving him a pat on the shoulder before returning to his post in the corner.

The other guys, who'd been strangely quiet during the whole scuffle, resumed their usual midgame chatter. Cade took a seat at the far end of the bench, away from his teammates, wondering what the hell had just happened.

He wasn't a violent guy, typically. Laid-back and

easygoing, that was Cade Hardesty. The guy least likely to lose his temper.

So why had he lost it on O'Brien?

Okay, the jerk-wad had insulted Ivy. Called her fat. It wasn't anything Cade hadn't heard a million times from the kids in school. They even had some dumb-ass, humiliating nickname for her, something about Jabba the Hutt. But he hadn't gone around threatening to beat the shit out of every kid who used it.

Of course, he'd been nothing but a stupid, self-centered kid himself back then. All he'd cared about was who he could con into doing his chemistry homework and which chick he was going to take to Hotchkiss Point on a Friday night. He'd like to think he was past that now. Maybe that's why he'd leaped to Ivy's defense at last.

Cade watched as O'Brien swung and missed. Strike two. Not surprising. The guy must be blind if he thought Ivy was fat. Hadn't he ever seen Jennifer Lopez? Or Kim Kardashian? There was a big difference between overweight and curvy. And Ivy most definitely fell into the curvy category.

He leaned his head against the dugout wall and closed his eyes, remembering how those soft curves had felt molded against him from chest to thigh. She was all sun-kissed, satiny skin. And that kiss…damn. He'd been hard from the minute her mouth met his.

"Wake up, man." A hand jostled his shoulder. "O'Brien grounded out. We're in the field."

Cade jammed his cap on his head, grabbed his glove ~~d trotted out to third base. Once he was in position, ~~ed a glance at the stands. Even in a crowd, Ivy ~~to spot. She'd positioned herself front and center in the first row. Her ponytail bobbed wildly as she nodded her head to the beat of the Springsteen song playing over the PA.

She looked up as the song ended. They might be sixty feet apart, but that didn't stop Cade's insides from somersaulting when her eyes met his. The unfamiliar emotion was like an itch he couldn't scratch.

"Heads up, Hardesty."

Cade pivoted toward the voice, silently thanking the powers that be for the interruption. The shortstop tossed him the ball, and Cade wheeled and threw it home, completing the circuit.

"Looking good, baby." Sasha stood in her seat and waved so enthusiastically her bought-and-paid-for boobs almost bounced out of her practically nonexistent top.

"Yeah, baby," O'Brien mocked from across the diamond, pursing his lips and making goo-goo eyes at Cade. "Looking good."

Cade scuffed at the dirt around third base with the toe of his cleat. They were down by three in the fourth. He had one woman he couldn't handle and another he'd like to but damn well shouldn't. And that no-necked goon O'Brien seemed hell-bent on pissing him off.

It was going to be a long freaking night.

4

"NICE GAME," CADE repeated through gritted teeth as he went down the line of police officers, shaking hands. Christ, he hated losing. Especially when it was his own damn fault.

"Better luck next year." The last cop in line squeezed Cade's hand a little too hard, his smile a little too broad.

"Bite me." Cade squeezed right back, engaging his long-time friend and one-time roommate Trey Brannigan in a familiar battle of wills.

"No, thanks." Trey grimaced but held on. "But I will bite into at least four slices of Valentino's meat-lovers special, courtesy of the SFD."

"Keep it up and it may just be your last meal."

Cappy came up behind Cade and clapped his shoulder. "Play nice, boys."

"We were just messing around, Cap." Cade dropped Trey's hand.

His buddy smirked at him, barely suppressing a laugh, and mouthed, *I win.*

"Well, quit messing around." Cappy thrust an equipment bag at Cade and gestured to the balls, bats and gloves strewn on the ground around home plate and near the dugouts. "You struck out three times tonight, more than anyone else on the team. That means you get to pick up the gear. And don't forget the bases."

Cappy strode off, and Cade turned back to his friend. "Looks like I'm gonna be a while. Save me a seat at Valentino's."

"Don't you mean three?" Trey looked over Cade's shoulder.

Cade followed Trey's gaze and saw Sasha and Ivy bearing down on him from opposite directions. "Shit. Can you run interference for me?"

"Which one do you want me to waylay?" Trey snickered. "The blonde or the redhead?"

"The blonde. Keep her busy while Ivy and I grab the equipment and run."

"Ivy?" Trey squinted at her. "Damn. Is that Jabba the Mutt?"

There was that stupid nickname again. Cade clenched his fists at his sides. "Don't call her that."

"Sorry, man." Trey stepped back, holding his hands up, palms out, in a show of surrender. "I didn't realize things were like that."

Cade frowned. "Like what?"

"When a guy rushes to his woman's defense, he's hooked. Not that I blame you. If I'd known she was gonna turn out this hot, I would've paid more attention to her in high school."

"I don't have time to argue with you." Cade's eyes pinged from Ivy to Sasha. Both women were gunning for him like a couple of F-14 fighter jets. He turned to Trey, just shy of begging. "Will you get Sasha off my back or not?"

"Damn. You've got Jabba the…"

Cade gave his friend a murderous look, stopping Trey in midsentence before he corrected himself.

"…Ivy *and* the Gibson's girl after you?" Trey whistled. "Lucky stiff."

Stiff didn't even begin to describe how he'd feel after those two were through with him. And not in a good way. "Yes or no?"

"Fine." Trey headed off to intercept Sasha, calling over his shoulder as he went, "You owe me one."

Cade was tempted to respond that distracting Sasha wasn't much of a hardship. After all, she was blonde and beautiful, with a killer rack and legs that went on for days. But she was also self-centered and not too bright. And at a certain point in a guy's life, the pretty package wasn't enough to outweigh the personality flaws.

He was definitely at that point. He wasn't so sure about Trey.

"Geez, you weren't kidding about your ex," Ivy said as she approached him. "That girl can't take a hint to save her life."

Cade took her elbow and ushered her toward home plate. "You can tell me all about it later. Right now we've got to pick up this gear and get out of here before Sasha figures out Trey's blowing smoke up her ass."

"Trey Brannigan, from high school?"

Ivy seemed to shrink before his eyes. He tried to ignore the lump of guilt in his stomach. He'd been her friend back then, but when push came to shove he was no better than the assholes who'd ridiculed her. Like Trey.

Fortunately, most people grew out of that bullshit. For the most part Trey had, although once in a while he slipped back into his old ways, which usually earned him a smack upside the head from Cade.

"Trey can be an idiot. But the ladies love him. He'll keep Sasha out of our hair until we can split." He handed her the bag. "I'll pull up the bases if you get the equipment."

"No problem." She went right to work. Yet another difference between her and Sasha, who would have made some excuse about ruining her designer duds or breaking a nail.

Not that the comparison mattered. Because he wasn't any more interested in Ivy than he was in Sasha. Despite her obvious charms. Charms that were on full display as she bent to gather the gear in that tied-too-tight shirt and shorter-than-short shorts.

It took him twice as long as it should have to pry up the bases thanks to the repeated glimpses of Ivy's ample cleavage and biteable bottom. When he was done, he met her behind the backstop, where she was zipping up the bag.

"All set."

"I'll get that." He reached for the bag as she hefted it over her shoulder.

"Are you kidding?" She shook him off and started for the parking lot, not even breaking a sweat. "You've seen the stuff I work with, right? I haul around twice this much every day."

"I thought you had people to do that for you."

"Not always."

She hitched up the bag, and for the first time he realized what had struck him about her in the studio. Not so much that she was thinner than he remembered her, but that she was stronger.

No, that wasn't right, either. It was a strength inside, not just physically, that hadn't been there before.

"Quit dawdling," she called to him, not missing a step.

"Right behind you."

He jogged a few paces to catch up and they walked to his SUV in silence.

"Home free." Cade hit the button on his remote to unlock the doors.

"Hey, baby."

So damn close, but yet so fucking far.

Sasha's high heels crunched in the gravel as she bore down on them across the parking lot. "Wait up."

"So much for your diversionary tactic." Ivy tossed the equipment bag onto the backseat. "Guess Trey's not the ladies' man either of you think he is."

She slammed the door and turned to face him, hands on her hips in that way she had, the one that made her breasts strain against the fabric of her shirt, her nipples clearly visible under the SFD logo. He cleared his throat and adjusted the crotch of his baseball pants.

"Come on." He reached for the car door handle. "We can still make it if we hurry. This puppy may not look like much, but it can go zero to sixty in under seven seconds."

"I've got a better idea." Ivy put a hand over his, stopping him from opening the door. "Kiss me."

His breath caught in his throat. "What?"

"Are you deaf or dense?" She leaned in to him, pressing those damn delicious breasts against his chest. "Kiss. Me. Like you mean it. If that doesn't convince her you're not interested, nothing will."

He took a step back and found himself pinned between Ivy's soft, warm curves and the cold, hard SUV. Not much of a dilemma there except for the whole safe-distance thing. "I thought that was a last resort."

"What's more last-resort than her closing in on us like a heat-seeking missile? It's why you brought me here, isn't it? What we practiced for." She molded herself to him and he was pretty sure she could feel his erection against her thigh. "One little kiss and she'll get the message."

"And what message is that, exactly?"

With surprising force, she grabbed his shoulders and spun him around so she was the one trapped against the car. She rose up on tiptoe so when she spoke her lips moved against his.

"This one."

THEIR FIRST KISS was a brushfire compared to this. This was a five-alarm inferno.

Last time Ivy had gone in with the intent to tease, to tantalize. This time she was more like a one-woman wrecking crew, determined to wipe thoughts of Sasha or any other woman from Cade's mind.

Only he wasn't biting. Literally or figuratively.

She slid her lips along his strong jaw, smiling as she tasted him. Salt and soap and all sorts of yummy maleness. Just like she'd imagined since she hit puberty.

"This isn't supposed to be a solo performance," she whispered against his neck. The sweet scrape of his five-o'-clock shadow made her lips tingle. "Do something. Put your hand on my ass. Your tongue down my throat. Anything."

He mumbled something that sounded like "fuck safe distance," wedged a leg between hers and cupped her ass, dragging her to him. She sighed into the hollow at the base of his neck and reached around to pull his shirt from the waistband of his pants.

"That's more like it." She slipped her hands under his shirt and up his back, still slick with sweat from the ball game, scraping gently with her nails as she went. He rewarded her with a shudder and her insides did a little happy dance. He might want to deny it, but he was as affected by this as she was. The evidence was undeniable, pressing against her core.

"Christ, Ivy." He moaned, further proving her point.

Over his shoulder she saw Sasha. Her steps had slowed and her mouth gaped as she stared at them.

"Perfect. She's looking at us like she's seen the Ghost of Christmas Past. Kiss me and she'll probably keel over."

"Then it's a good thing there's plenty of cops and firefighters around," Cade murmured just before his mouth claimed hers. His hands left her bottom and traveled up to frame her face. In one swift but gentle move, he tugged off her baseball cap and freed her hair from the ponytail, letting it cascade over his fingers.

A moan stuck in Ivy's throat as his lips teased and pressed harder. She opened to him, letting his tongue play with hers in a dance as old as time but new to her. Sure, she'd kissed guys before. Not many, but a few. And not like this. Hot. Wet. Urgent.

She melted into him, her legs unable to support her weight. His big hand trailed down her neck, his fingers toying with the top button of the borrowed baseball jersey, teasing the sensitive skin between her breasts and making her shiver.

He broke off the kiss and licked a moist path to her ear, his teeth tugging at the lobe. "Sasha still watching?"

Sasha who?

"Uh-huh." The two syllables were all Ivy could manage.

"She look convinced?" His breath stirred the hair behind her ear, and he raised a hand to twine a strand around his finger.

It took a second for Ivy to come out of her lust-induced haze so she could focus on the parking lot beyond Cade's shoulder. Sasha was at a dead stop a few feet away, hands on her model-thin hips, eyes flashing. She met Ivy's gaze, tossed her perfectly coiffed, long, blond hair in a gesture that screamed "I have no clue why he's with you when he could have all of this" and stomped off.

"She looks pissed. Or looked. She's gone now."

"Good." He let his hand drop and reached around her to open the car door. "Your chariot awaits."

"Valentino's?" she asked, still shaking a bit from the aftereffects of their kiss as she climbed in. "I'm dying for a piece of meat-lovers pie. Or three."

She cringed, instantly regretting mentioning her appetite—another knee-jerk reaction from her way overweight days, when talk of food had been all but verboten—but Cade didn't seem to notice. He leaned on the open door. "Sasha's bound to be there. Sure you're up for that?"

After that kiss, she wasn't sure of anything, especially her ability to be within five feet of Cade without mauling him like a sex-starved grizzly. But at least at Valentino's they'd be surrounded by a crowd. And dinner would put off the awkwardness when he dropped her off at the end of the night.

"I'm game as long as you are."

"Great." He bent to pick up her baseball cap, brushed it off and handed it to her. "I'm starving."

Two hours, one beer and more pieces of pizza than she wanted to admit later, Ivy yawned, unable to delay the inevitable any longer. She tapped Cade, who was sitting next to her, on the shoulder. "Can we leave soon? I've got to be at the nursery at the butt crack of dawn, and it's way past my bedtime."

Plus, she'd had about as much of Sasha and her high-pitched, fake laugh as she could take. Cade's ex had kept her distance, but that annoying laugh traveled across the room like a bullet to the brain.

And then there were the well-meaning but double-edged compliments from classmates she hadn't seen since graduation.

"Oh, my God, Ivy, is that you?"

"What happened to you?"

"You're so much thinner."

And her personal favorite: "Are you sick?" Like that was the only conceivable way Jabba the Mutt could drop a few pounds.

Cade pulled out his wallet. "No problem. I'm ready to head out, too."

He threw a handful of bills on the table and stood. "This ought to cover my share."

Trey snatched it up. "If it doesn't, I'll be sure to let you know."

"Thanks for everything," Cade said to Ivy once they'd gotten into his SUV. "I owe you."

"We're even, remember?" She ran a finger along the brim of the ball cap, now laying in her lap. "The dare."

"Right. The dare." He turned onto the narrow road that circled Leffert's Pond and led to Holly and Nick's place. "Anyway, you were great tonight."

Ivy stared silently out the window, her heart knocking against her ribs. He had no idea how great tonight could be, if only she could work up the nerve. After a few minutes, she turned to Cade, his profile handsome even in the eerie half light of the car's dashboard. She wished she had her Nikon so she could capture him. "So, that kiss…"

"Yeah, that was something." He shot her a quick, embarrassed smile and her heart skittered even faster. "I bet I won't be hearing from Sasha again after that performance."

Screech. Just like that, her heart skidded to a stop, her hopes dashed.

Performance? Who did he think was performing? Her? Him? Both of them?

She scrunched up the baseball cap in her hands. "That's not the word I'd use to describe it."

"Why not?"

"For your information, Mr. I'm-Too-Sexy-For-My-Turnouts Hardesty, I was not 'performing.'" She made air quotes around the last word. "And neither were you, if the hard-on jabbing against me was anything to go by."

He shrugged. "What can I say? I'm a guy. It's a natural reaction when a woman plasters herself against you and kisses you like a porn star."

"A woman?" She leaned against the car door, increasing the distance between them. "Any woman?"

Cade didn't answer. Instead, he pulled into the driveway, jamming the gearshift into Park but not turning off the engine.

Ivy got the message, loud and clear. As far as he was concerned the night—and their conversation—was over. The second she got out of the car he'd make his escape. But she wasn't giving up that easy.

She settled into her seat and crossed her arms. "So you're telling me you're not the least bit attracted to me?"

"We've known each other for ages. I'm your brother's best friend."

"That doesn't answer my question."

He ran a hand through his honey-blond hair, something she'd longed to do for what seemed like an eternity.

"It's a damn good thing Gabe's in New York. If he caught us, he'd have beaten the shit out of me." Cade smirked. "Or tried."

Ivy glared at him. "If you hadn't noticed, I'm all grown up. Gabe has nothing to do with this. With us."

"There is no *us*." He said the last word like it was one of the little brown nuggets the Canadian geese left on the lakeshore.

"Don't get all commitment-phobic on me. I'm not talking me in a white gown and you in your dress blues. I'm blowing this Popsicle stand as soon as Dad's back on his feet. But in the meantime we're clearly hot for each other. We've got an itch. Who says we can't scratch it?"

"Me." He reached across her for the door handle.

She stopped him with a hand on his forearm. "Think of it as added insurance against another messy confrontation with Sasha."

"There's a big difference between making her think we're an item and ruining our friendship by jumping in the sack together."

"Is that what you're worried about? Our friendship? We've barely spoken to each other in years."

Her own fault, she knew, for staying away so long, but still an indisputable fact. Her grip on his arm tightened, the soft hairs tickling her palm. She wondered if the hair on his chest was as silky. Or the treasure trail leading down to his waistband…and below.

Cade jerked back as if he could read the direction of her thoughts.

"Friends don't have to talk on the phone every day to stay close," he insisted, his voice sincere. "And that's what we are, right? Friends."

Great. Friend-zoned again. The curse of the full-figured gal. Guys took one look at her and immediately put her on the do-not-date list.

"Fine, friend." The last word dripped with sarcasm and tears threatened to spill down her cheeks. She blinked to keep them at bay. She'd been fifty times a fool thinking a little makeup and some revealing clothes would make Cade see her as a desirable woman and not the fat chick always snapping pictures for the high school yearbook. Okay, so his dick had noticed. But not his head. Or his heart.

The parts that mattered to her.

No, no, no. This wasn't about heads or hearts. She was leaving in a few weeks. He was staying. All it was about—all it ever could be about—was down-and-dirty, no-strings-attached, good-enough-to-last-the-rest-of-your-lifetime sex.

Too bad he didn't see it that way.

With jerky movements, she unbuttoned the borrowed jersey. "See you around. Good luck with Sasha.

She doesn't strike me as a woman who takes 'no' lying down."

"Ivy, wait…"

But she'd waited long enough for Cade Hardesty. Sixteen years, to be exact, since grade school, when she'd started to notice things about her brother's best buddy. Like his full, firm, oh-so-kissable lips and his solid-looking chest with the dusting of hair she saw when he took his shirt off in the summer and God, oh, God, the vee at his hips pointing to nirvana that made her brain freeze.

Her palms sweaty, she took off his shirt, balled it up and threw it at him, leaving her half-naked in her sports bra. But he sure as hell didn't care, and neither did she. "Here. I'd offer to wash it, but I'm sure you'll find some other friend to help you out."

Before he could respond, she'd gotten out of the SUV, slammed the door shut and was heading up the stone walkway to the front door. She fumbled for her keys and heard gravel spin out from under his tires as he backed out of the driveway then sped off down the street.

She almost laughed at the irony of it. She'd just dumped a man who refused to go out with her.

5

If he lived to be a hundred, Cade would never understand women. Especially one feisty, curvy redhead who'd been taking up way too much space in his brain the past few weeks.

All he'd said was the truth. They were friends. Was it so wrong that he didn't want to risk their relationship for a night of doing the horizontal mambo? Even if, based on the heat generated by their kisses, it would probably be the stuff sexual legends were made of.

He shook his head and reached for the extra virgin olive oil. It was his turn to cook for the squad, and he was trying pasta with clam sauce. Maybe focusing on his culinary skills—or lack thereof—would take his mind off how Ivy's lips felt on his, soft and sensuous, or how goddamn hard he'd gotten when she'd raked her nails down his back.

He tossed some minced garlic into the pan and stirred it with a wooden spoon, but his thoughts kept spinning back to Ivy and the scene in her driveway. She should be flattered that their friendship meant more to him than a night of meaningless, albeit mind-blowing, sex, not pissed off and refusing to return his calls or texts.

Unless what she had in mind was more than a meaningless one-night stand…

"What's burning?" Cappy barked. "We're supposed to put out fires, not start them."

"Shit." Cade pulled the pan off the burner and stared at the charred bits of garlic.

Cappy wrinkled his nose. "Please tell me that wasn't dinner."

"It was." Cade strode to the sink, turned on the faucet and stuck the pan underneath. "Good news is it's not too late to start over."

"What's with you lately, son?" Cappy grabbed a bottle of water out of the fridge and sat down at the enormous oak slab table with the station's logo embossed in the center that took up most of the firehouse kitchen. "Your head hasn't been in the game since the Battle of the Badges. You're not still upset we lost, are you?"

"Nah."

"O'Brien still bugging you? I can give him a verbal warning."

"Not necessary, Cap." Cade finished rinsing the pan, stuck it back on the stove and began chopping fresh garlic. "We're cool."

As "cool" as they were going to get, unless O'Brien made another crack about Ivy. Then all bets were off.

Cappy cracked open his water bottle and took a sip. "If work's not the problem, it must be something at home. You got woman trouble? Maybe one of those gals at the game?"

The knife slipped in Cade's hand, almost slicing off

the tip of his index finger. *Jesus Christ.* Did they have to talk about this now? Or ever?

"Look, Hardesty," Cappy continued. Apparently they did have to talk about this. "You're one of my best men. But you're no good to me or anyone else in the company stumbling around like something out of *The Walking Dead.*"

A stab of guilt pierced Cade in the gut. Cappy was right. Cade was damn lucky the most serious call they'd had in the past week was from a lady whose five-year-old somehow got her head stuck between the toilet and the wall. With the way he'd been acting, he'd have risked his own life and the lives of all his brothers in arms in an actual fire.

He put down the knife and turned to his captain. "I'm sorry. I'll pull my head out of my ass, I promise."

"See that you do." Cappy gave him a dismissive nod, indicating the conversation was blessedly over, and Cade turned back to the garlic.

"Do what?" O'Brien came in from the engine bay, followed by Sykes and Hansen, B Company's paramedics. "Cook dinner without burning it? Smells like it's too late for that."

"Lay off." Cappy pushed his chair back and stood, slapping a palm on the table. "Let the man work."

They disappeared, leaving Cade to mince and dice in peace. About half an hour later, just as he was pouring the sauce over the pasta, the alarm blared.

"Figures," he muttered, shoving an uncovered bowl of salad into the fridge. "I knew we'd never get to eat it hot. It smelled too damn good."

He dropped the now-empty pan into the sink, double-checked the burners to make sure they were off and raced to the lockers, where the rest of the crew was already jumping into their turnout gear.

"What's the deal?" O'Brien asked as he pulled on his boots.

"Ten twenty-six," Cappy answered, clapping his helmet on his head. "Kitchen fire at 195 Leffert's Pond Road."

Cade froze, one leg in his bunkers and one out. "What was that address?"

"195 Leffert's Pond Road." Cappy slammed his locker shut and sprinted toward the engine bay.

"What's wrong, man?" Hansen shrugged on his jacket. "You look like you've been hit by a bus."

"I'm good." Cade jerked on his pants, pulled up his suspenders and stepped into his boots.

"You don't look good," O'Brien chimed in. "You look like shit."

"I said I'm good." Cade grabbed his coat and helmet. "Let's roll."

He spun on his heel and ran after Cappy, not wanting his fellow firefighters to see what a goddamn liar he was. Because he wasn't good. He was just about the furthest thing you could be from good.

195 Leffert's Pond Road was the old Pagano place. The place Nick had bought for Holly when they'd gotten engaged. The place where Ivy was staying while she was in town.

If there was a time to pull his head out of his ass, it was now.

Ivy DIDN'T KNOW whether to be relieved or mortified when she heard the sirens.

Relieved because it meant help would get there before the pot of pasta on the stove went up in flames and burned the whole house down. Mortified because she was stuck halfway through the doggy door, her spandex-clad ass hanging out for the whole darned world to see.

Okay, it was her own stupid fault for locking herself out of the house with dinner cooking. She'd just gone to grab the mail, and the evening had barreled downhill from there. It was like a comedy of errors—the door locking behind her, her cell sitting useless on the kitchen counter, the only neighbor in spitting distance not at home and, finally, her fateful decision to squeeze through the doggy door.

The acrid smell of smoldering spaghetti filled her nostrils. *Fudge bucket.* With all the water gone, the pasta was burning to the bottom of the pot, about to burst into flames.

Good thing Nick had sprung for a fancy alarm system that called 9-1-1 when the smoke detector went off. But where was the fire department?

The sirens grew closer. Finally, after what seemed like a lifetime of staring at the Clean Up After Yourself, House Elves Don't Work Here needlepoint hanging over the washer/dryer in the mudroom, the crunch of gravel in the driveway, followed by shouts and door slams, told Ivy the firefighters had arrived.

She took a deep breath to steady her jangling nerves, but only succeeded in irritating herself thanks to the stinging smell. Coughing, she blinked her watery eyes, opening them in time to see a pair of black-and-yellow boots on the tile floor directly in front of her.

"Uh, hey, Ivy."

Her gaze traveled up long legs, past a trim waist to a familiar, broad chest, all protected by turnout gear.

"Going in or out?" Cade quipped with a smirk.

"Very funny." Ivy blew a wisp of hair out of her eyes. "How about taking care of the conflagration about to erupt on my stove? That's your job, right?"

"O'Brien's on it." He kneeled down so they were more at eye level. "Do you think I'd be here calmly making small talk if you were still in danger?"

"I was not in danger." *Much.*

"Are you kidding?" His eyes flashed. "You're damn lucky it wasn't worse—which it would have been if it wasn't for the state-of-the art security system Nick had installed. As it is, you'll have to ventilate the kitchen for a few days to get rid of the smell. And you owe your sister and her husband a new saucepan. But that's the extent of it."

He tilted his head to study the half of her that had made it into the house. "Well, that and the fact that you're stuck in the doggy door."

She consoled herself with the thought that he was inside, not on the porch talking to her ass.

"Yeah, about that…" She held her hands out. "Could you, maybe, pull me out of here or something?"

He sat on his very fine butt, bracing his feet against the door on either side of her, and grabbed her forearms. As embarrassed as she was, she couldn't stop the hum of pleasure that buzzed through her at his touch.

"Ready?" he asked, his gaze boring into hers. "On three."

She swallowed hard and nodded.

"One…two…three."

He pulled. She stayed.

"Hmm." He released her and wiped his hands on his bunker pants. "You're really wedged in there."

She rolled her eyes. "Tell me something I don't know, Captain Obvious."

Another firefighter, who Ivy recognized from the softball game as the company captain, appeared behind Cade, followed by two more.

A bigger audience. Fan-freaking-tastic.

"The rest of the house is all clear," Cappy announced.

"Need some help rescuing your girlfriend?" one of the others asked. "Or are you with the blonde this week? I can't keep your women straight."

"Zip it, O'Brien," Cappy barked. "And get in line."

In a matter of seconds, they'd formed a human chain with Cade at the front and the guy Cappy called O'Brien as the anchor.

"Hold on tight," Cade said, gripping her arms again. "Like last time. On three."

"Shouldn't we have someone push from—pardon the pun—behind?" O'Brien's voice reeked of snark.

"I hate to admit it, but that's not a bad idea." Cappy pulled his radio out of his belt and pressed the button. "Sykes. Send a team around back. We've got a female trapped in the pet door and need some pushing power."

Pushing power? What was she? Fudgie the Whale?

Oh, wait, she'd almost forgotten. In this town, she'd always be Jabba the Mutt, no matter how long she'd been gone or how much weight she'd lost. Precisely why she'd stayed away for almost thirteen years. And why she was leaving the minute her father was back in top form.

"Ready out here, Cap," a voice crackled over the radio.

"Okay, like Cade said, on three." Cappy returned to his place in line. "One…"

She felt a pair of hands on her ass. Could this possibly get any more humiliating?

"Two…"

She let out a squeak as the hands shifted, hopefully to find a better pushing position and not to cop a cheap feel.

"Enjoying yourself?" Cade quirked a brow.

Oh, yeah. It could get more humiliating.

"Hardly." She closed her eyes to escape his teasing smile.

"Three."

Grunts and groans, mixed with an occasional expletive, filled the room. She felt like a chew toy caught between two rottweilers as the firefighters tugged and shoved.

"That's it."

"She's coming free."

"Almost there."

"One more and she's out."

With a *pop*, Ivy sprang loose, landing like a wet rag in Cade's lap. She forced her eyes open to see him looking down at her with a shit-eating grin.

"Nice catch," she muttered, scrambling off him.

"They don't call me Sure Hands Hardesty for nothing."

"I've never heard anyone call you that."

He shrugged. "They should."

Ivy didn't doubt that. And not just because of his prowess in rescue situations. She shuddered, remembering the way those hands had brought her to a fever pitch during their kisses, kneading her ass, framing her face, molding her breasts.

"Clear away from the door," Cappy ordered, snapping her out of her trance. "Let the paramedics in."

"I'm fine, honest." She stood gingerly and brushed herself off. "Nothing wounded except my pride."

"Department protocol says we need to examine you."

"I'll sign a waiver." Anything to get them the heck out of there.

"Would you be more comfortable if I did the exam?" Cade rose, first addressing her then turning to his captain. "I've got my EMT certification."

She blushed, thinking of those hands roaming over her body again, creating ripples of sweet sensation.

Hell to the no.

Before she could voice her objection, Cappy spoke up.

"Okay by me." The door cracked open and a man in a paramedic uniform carrying a duffel bag entered. "Sykes, give Hardesty your BLS bag."

"Sure, Cap." The paramedic handed the duffel to Cade, who ushered Ivy onto the built-in storage bench and kneeled on the floor beside her, unzipping the bag and pulling out a blood pressure cuff.

"Stay with Hardesty while he completes his exam." Cappy took off his helmet and wiped his forehead with the back of his hand.

"Yes, sir." Sykes nodded.

Once everyone else had gone, Cade worked quickly and efficiently, poking and prodding Ivy until he was satisfied there was no damage done.

"Looks like everything's intact." He zipped the bag shut and stood.

"Told you so." She stuck her tongue out at him.

Sykes picked up the duffel and slung it over his shoulder. "My patients are usually more grateful. Is she always this fresh? Or is it just your crappy bedside manner?"

"It's just him." Ivy gave Sykes her sweetest smile. "I'm really a pussycat."

"More like a tiger," Cade muttered. "Who's not afraid to use her claws."

"So are you done with me or what?" She stood and faced off with him, hands on her hips. He wanted claws, he'd get claws. "I'm starving."

"You might want to give the stove the night off," Sykes suggested. "Your kitchen kind of stinks to high heaven. Hu Nan Pan delivers. Or I could bring something back for you. My shift's over in an hour."

"I need a minute with Ivy." Cade's voice was low but firm.

"Go ahead." Sykes stared him down, white-knuckling the strap of the duffel bag. "Take all the time you need."

"Alone," Cade growled, fists clenched.

Goody, goody. Alpha males engaging in ritualized aggressive behavior to assert dominance. Nice to know she could still remember her freshman intro to human psychology class.

"Fine." Sykes loosened his grip on the strap ever so slightly. "I'll open some windows to air the place out and wait for you in the rig. Ivy, my offer still stands. Call me at the station if you're craving something other than Chinese."

"Thanks. I might just do that."

As soon as Sykes was out of earshot, Cade turned his attention—and his anger—on Ivy. "What do you mean 'you might just do that?'"

"Why not?" Ivy lifted a shoulder in a half-hearted shrug. "I'm single. He's single. And we've both got to eat."

"How can you even think about food after what happened here tonight?" Cade crossed his arms. His large frame, made even larger by the bulky turnout gear, seemed to take up all the space and all the oxygen in the tiny mudroom. "Do you realize you could have died?"

"Melodramatic much?"

"You don't even have a fire extinguisher in the kitchen, for Christ's sake. And when was the last time you cleaned the stove?"

"It's not my fault Holly and Nick don't own a fire extinguisher. I'll run right out and get one. Cross my heart."

"I'm not joking, Ivy. Safety is serious business."

She narrowed her eyes at him. "Are you telling me that as a firefighter or as a friend?"

"Both."

Not the answer she wanted. She would have preferred something like, "I'm telling you as the man who's always been secretly in love with you." Or even, "I'm telling you as the man who wants to screw you senseless."

No such luck.

"That's what I thought." She squeezed past him into the kitchen, trying hard to ignore the way her breasts tingled when she brushed against him.

"What did I say wrong now?" he asked, following her.

"If you don't know, I'm not going to tell you." Okay, it was juvenile. But she was way past giving a flying fig. She grabbed the ruined pot, dropped it into the sink and filled it with water.

"Then how am I supposed to fix it?" He leaned against the counter next to her, so close she could smell the citrusy scent of his aftershave even over the burned pasta.

"You're not." She picked up a sponge and moved back to the stove to put some distance between them. "You can't. This is about me, not you."

The radio on his belt sputtered. "Engine five, rescue

one. Code three. Ten twenty-four at the intersection of Jefferson and Grand. Please respond."

"Shit. I've got to go."

"Code three, is that bad? Is it dangerous?" *Crap.* Why did she go there? She didn't want him thinking she'd be up all night worrying about him. Even if it was true.

"Car fire." He headed for the door.

"We're not through here," he called over his shoulder. "I'll call you later."

"You do that," she said to his back.

Maybe she'd pick up. Maybe she'd be busy with Sykes. Or maybe she'd just crawl under the covers with a good book, preferably something with a happily-ever-after, and escape from the real world.

Again.

6

IT WAS PITCH-BLACK when Cade went back to Nick and Holly's place that night, hat in hand. Or, more accurately, fire extinguisher in hand, along with a whole host of home security essentials, including a flashlight, first-aid kit and fresh batteries for the smoke detectors.

Nothing said "I'm sorry" like fire safety equipment, even though he didn't have a clue exactly what he was apologizing for. All he knew was he didn't like the uncomfortable feeling he got in the pit of his stomach when Ivy was upset with him.

He turned off the ignition and hit the overhead light so he could look at his watch—10:25 p.m. Was that too late? He wasn't privy to Ivy's sleeping habits. He clicked off the overhead and stared at the semidark house, feeling a little like a crazed stalker, if crazed stalkers came bearing carbon monoxide alarms.

He was about to bail when a light flicked on in the bay window. So Ivy was awake. No excuse for chickening out now.

Juggling his Home Depot bags, Cade climbed out of his SUV and rang the doorbell. A second later, Ivy opened the door wearing a V-necked What the f/Stop T-shirt that clung to her obviously braless breasts and a pair of loose, pink-and-yellow plaid sleep pants that shouldn't have been so sexy.

"A little late for a social call, isn't it?" she asked, hanging on the half-open door.

He held up the bags. "Am I forgiven if I brought gifts?"

She eyed the bright orange Home Depot logo. "I take it it's not flowers or candy."

"Nope." He smiled. "Something longer-lasting."

"A hacksaw? Socket set? Cordless drill?"

"Let me in and you'll see."

"Okay." She stood back and let him pass. "But only because I'm a sucker for power tools."

He went into the kitchen, put the bags on the butcher-block counter and started pulling items out one by one. Setting them down with a flourish, he said, "Sorry, no power tools today. Maybe next time."

Ivy scowled. "I told you I'd get my own fire extinguisher."

"Hey." He held up a hand, palm out. "This is a peace offering, not a declaration of war."

"A peace offering implies we're already at war."

"Aren't we?" He pulled out an eight-pack of AA batteries and leaned back, arms braced against the counter. "You've been freezing me out since the ball game."

She slid to the floor, her back to the row of cabinets opposite him, and hugged her pink-and-yellow-clad legs to her chest. "About that…"

"Me first." He sat down next to her, suppressing a smile at her slippers. Fluffy neon-green frogs with bulging eyes and broad smiles. She may have changed a little on the outside, but inside she was still the same funny, spunky, self-assured girl who had staged a sit-in when the school board tried to cut the high school jazz band.

Qualities he'd been too superficial to appreciate as a teen. But he wasn't superficial now. So why was he resisting what she'd so willingly offered?

Because it wasn't just her he stood to lose. It was Gabe. Holly. Noelle. Their parents. The closest thing to a real family he'd ever known.

Cade turned his head and met Ivy's clear, gray-green gaze. "I know things have been awkward between us since our kiss."

One corner of her mouth lifted. "Don't you mean kisses?"

"If you want to get technical."

"I do."

He scrubbed a hand through his hair, still damp at the ends from the shower he'd taken when he got off duty. "You're not going to make this easy for me, are you?"

She shrugged. "You want easy, there's always Sasha."

He grimaced. "Been there, done that, burned the T-shirt."

Ivy laughed, and just like that the tension between them deflated.

"So are we okay?" Cade asked. "You gonna stop avoiding me?"

"I have not been avoiding you."

"Bullshit." He held out a hand. "Let me see your cell. Guaranteed there's at least ten unanswered calls from me and probably twice that many texts you ignored."

She smacked his hand away. "Fine. I'll stop avoiding you. On one condition."

"What's that?"

"Stop treating me like your best friend's pain-in-the-ass sister."

"You're not a pain in the ass."

She laughed again, a sweet, soft, musical sound that made his chest tighten. "Now who's bullshitting?"

"You're not," he insisted. "But you *are* my best friend's sister."

She sighed and closed her eyes, leaning her head back against the cabinets and exposing the long line of her neck, a line he wanted to trace with his tongue from her ear to her collarbone. "Couldn't you conveniently forget that for, like, an hour or so?"

"An hour?" Now it was his turn to chuckle. "You underestimate me."

Her eyes shot open, pinning him with a heated stare. "Are you flirting with me?"

He shouldn't be, dammit. His head knew it was a bad idea. But majority ruled, apparently, and the rest of him, especially the region south of his belt buckle, was screaming for him to quit stalling and give the lady what she wanted. "Maybe."

"Don't promise what you're not willing to deliver."

"Don't ask for what you're not willing to take."

"So that's how you want to play it." Without warning, she kicked off her fuzzy slippers and climbed into his lap, straddling him. "I've never been the aggressor before, but there's always a first time."

He'd never been the aggressee before, either, but if she was game, so was he. Especially if it meant her crotch pressing into his stiffening cock and her breasts crushed against his chest, her nipples hardening to pinpoints under her T-shirt.

"What about Gabe?" he asked, half hoping that saying

his friend's name would snap him out of his lust-ridden stupor, half praying it wouldn't.

"Gabe who?" Ivy leaned in to brush a kiss across his lips, and her red-brown curls tumbled over her face, teasing his cheeks. "I thought you were going to forget him for the next hour."

"Or more." Cade buried his nose in her hair and breathed her in. Damn, she smelled good. Like sunshine and sugar cookies and the air after a warm spring rainstorm.

"More?" She arched her neck, inviting him to lick the path he'd just fantasized about. It was an invitation he wasn't strong enough to refuse, his relationship with her brother and the rest of her family be damned.

"Oh, yeah." He groaned against the soft skin of her throat, well past the point of no return. "Much more."

IT WAS FINALLY HAPPENING. After sixteen years, Ivy was finally going to have Cade Hardesty exactly where she wanted him.

In her bed.

Or, if the way he was frantically grasping for the bottom of her T-shirt was any indication, right there in the kitchen. And that was fine by her. And if she was lucky and he really did intend this to be more than a wham-bam kind of thing, maybe she'd have him in her bed before the night was over, too.

"Here, let me do that." She pulled her shirt over her head, leaving herself naked from the waist up and vulnerable. She was a far cry from the women she'd seen at his side in his Facebook photos. Her stomach wasn't exactly flat or her breasts perky. Instead of tossing the shirt aside, she held it to her chest.

"Don't. You. Dare." He punctuated each word with a kiss to her temple, her jaw and finally her lips. "There's a shortage of perfect breasts in this world. It would be a pity to hide yours."

"The Princess Bride." Slowly, she lowered the shirt. "You remembered."

"Of course I remembered." He pried the shirt from her hands and let it drop onto the tile floor beside him. "It was your favorite movie. You only made me watch it like once a week."

"Did not."

"Did too."

"Did—"

He silenced her with a hard, fast kiss. "I don't want to argue. Not when I've got these to play with."

He reached out and rubbed a finger over first one nipple then the other.

"No fair." She moaned.

"What?" He cupped her breast and squeezed. "You don't like this? Your nipples say otherwise."

"I like it just fine." She bit her lip, feeling suddenly shy. "But I'd like it even more if I could touch you, too."

"Who's stopping you?" His hand moved to her other breast, giving it the same treatment.

"Let me know if I'm doing something wrong," she whispered, pulling his shirt out of his pants and sliding it up his torso.

"Babe, if it involves you removing my clothes, there's no way it's wrong." He abandoned her breasts and she almost cried out in frustration until he raised his arms, allowing her to yank his shirt over his head, exposing the ripped pecs and abs that had been haunting her dreams since the calendar shoot.

She sucked in a breath and he gave her a self-satisfied smile. "Like what you see?"

"I'd have to be blind not to." She trailed a finger down the line bisecting his chest. "And even then, I could feel my way around."

He spread out his arms. "Help yourself."

He didn't have to tell her twice. She let her hands roam freely over his shoulders, his arms, his flat, hard stomach. She slipped them under his waistband and came dangerously close to the Promised Land until he grabbed her wrists and pinned them behind her back.

A frown wrinkled her forehead. "What's wrong?"

"I told you, babe. Nothing you do could be wrong."

"Then why did you stop me?"

"Because if you keep touching me like that, this will be over before it's started."

"Oh." She felt her cheeks redden. She wasn't a virgin by any means, but the sexual encounters she'd had were few and far between. And she sure as heck hadn't had the effect on any of the men involved that she seemed to be having on Cade.

"Yeah." He stared down at her, his blue eyes darkening almost to black, heavy with desire. "Oh."

"So what now?"

He lifted her arms over her head and gently lowered her to the floor. "Now you relax and let me take over for a while."

Relax? Was he kidding? He expected her to relax while he was sliding down her body, slipping off her sleep pants, spreading her out before him?

"Damn." He ran a finger around the bare folds of her pussy. "Smooth."

She said a silent thank-you to the Namibian model

who had introduced her waxing. Painful, sure. But the payoff…

She shuddered as Cade worked his finger inside her. "Please."

"Please what?" He buried his finger to the knuckle then withdrew it almost completely.

"Don't tease me." She squirmed under him, lifting her hips to follow his retreating digit.

"Patience, sweet thing." He splayed a hand across her abdomen, easing her back down. "You know what they say. Those who wait get to come good."

Sixteen years wasn't long enough?

"I think the expression is good things come to those who wait."

"Close enough." He lowered his head so that his lips hovered over her mound, his breath teasing the supersensitized flesh. "Now be a good girl and let me taste you."

Ivy almost shot up off the floor at the first lick of his tongue. And he hadn't even touched her clit. Instead, with the self-restraint of a goddamn saint, he honed in on her inner thighs, licking, sucking and nipping at the soft skin there. His finger continued to pulse inside her, thrusting once, twice, three times before he removed it, making her moan in protest.

"Patience," he repeated, raising his head to give her his trademark bad-boy grin. Slowly, agonizingly, his eyes not leaving hers, he lifted two fingers to his mouth and wetted them.

Holy Christmas. He wasn't touching her, but the sight of his fingers sliding in and out of his mouth was the most erotic thing she'd ever seen. She was practically ready to come just from watching him.

"Cade." She raised herself up on her elbows to see

better, not wanting to miss anything. She'd always preferred to close her eyes during sex, whether because she was afraid of what she'd see if she looked too deeply into her partner's eyes, or because she couldn't bear to look at herself naked, she wasn't sure.

Leave it to Cade to get her to release her inner voyeur.

She stared, panting as he ran one moist finger down her equally moist center then spread her open. With an almost primal growl, he lowered his head and her body stiffened, anticipating that first, delectable lick.

It was like being struck by lightning. Electrifying. Invigorating.

Terrifying.

He swept his tongue over her clit and her hips jerked upward. She clutched helplessly at the cold, hard tile beneath her as he toyed with the sensitive peak, alternatively swirling around it with his tongue and suckling it into his mouth. With each swirl and suckle, he brought her closer to the brink, taking her higher and higher until she felt like she was about to splinter into a thousand delicious pieces.

She squirmed and strained under him, desperate for her release. Her moans mingled with the lapping of his tongue and the ticking of the clock above the stove for what seemed like an eternity as he worked her to the edge then back down again.

"Dammit, Cade," she begged, past the point of politeness. "Let me come. I need to come."

She pressed her lips together, not wanting to say more. Like how long it had been since she'd had an orgasm that wasn't self-induced with a little help from her battery-operated boyfriend.

"Soon." He chuckled and the sound vibrated over her,

almost sending her spiraling. "You taste so damn sweet. I could do this all night."

"But what about you?" Ivy asked on a gasp, her body shuddering. "Don't you want to, you know, get off?"

"Don't worry, baby." He added his thumb to the mix, easing it inside her and stroking her gently. "I'll get off. But ladies first."

He delved back in, flicking her clit with his tongue while he slipped his thumb inside her once more. Her explosion was immediate and earth-shattering. Her hips bucked to meet him and her palms slapped the floor as she cried out his name.

When she'd drifted back to terra firma, he was looming over her, grinning like a happy puppy.

"I think I'm the one who's supposed to be smiling," she said, heat creeping up her cheeks. "You didn't even—"

"Get off?" he said with a wink. "Not yet, but I got to watch you, and that was pretty damn enjoyable."

"It was?"

"You have no idea." He brushed a lock of hair off her forehead. "The look on your face when you came. Knowing I put it there."

She gave his arm a playful push. "Egomaniac."

"What can I say?" In one fast, smooth motion, no doubt born from years of firefighting, he scooped her up and hoisted her over his shoulder. "I take pride in my work."

"Hey." She stared down at his butt, hugged lovingly by his well-worn jeans. You could bounce a quarter off that thing. "What are you doing?"

"Moving this party to the bedroom." He strode out

of the kitchen and up the stairs that led to the second floor. "Any objection?"

"Just one." His ass muscles bunched and flexed with each step under the faded denim, and she imagined peeling the fabric away and getting up close and personal. Maybe even bouncing that quarter. "We need to make a pit stop."

"A pit stop?"

"Second door on the left."

"What's that?"

"The bathroom." Ivy smiled at Cade's back. "There's condoms in the medicine cabinet."

7

CADE HAD NARROWLY escaped his share of burning buildings. But even with flames licking at his heels, he didn't think he'd ever moved this fast. Probably because saving his own ass hadn't seemed half as important as getting his hands on Ivy's.

After a quick detour for the condoms, she directed him to a door at the end of the hallway.

"This one?" he asked.

She nodded, and he kicked it open.

"Hey," she protested. "Be careful. Holly will kill me if we break anything."

He dropped her onto the wrought-iron bed and toed off his Vans. "I don't know. That thing doesn't look too sturdy."

She ran a hand over the patchwork quilt covering the mattress. "This was my great-grandmother's bed. It's been in the family for generations. I'm fairly certain it's seen plenty of action through the years."

He shucked off his socks and unbuttoned his jeans. "Trust me. It hasn't seen anything yet."

"Awfully sure of yourself, aren't you?"

"Sure of us." His pants and boxers joined his socks and shoes on the floor, and he stretched out next to her on the bed, both of them finally, blessedly naked. He wrapped his fingers around her ankle before sliding his hand up, over the slight swell of her belly, between her breasts, coming to rest in the hair at the nape of her neck, leaving a trail of goose bumps in his wake.

He took a minute to look at her before diving in. Her wider-than-wide gray-green eyes, flushed cheeks, full, begging-to-be kissed lips. She took a quick, sharp breath and he knew no matter what happened tomorrow, there, in that moment, she wanted him as much as he wanted her.

"Are you just going to lie there or are you going to do something?" she asked, confirming his thoughts.

"Oh, I'm going to do something, all right." He massaged her scalp while his other hand slid around to the small of her back. "I just wanted to look at you first. Get a good before picture."

"Before what?"

Before I kiss every single inch of you. Before I make us both come so hard we forget our own names. Before everything changes between us.

"Before this." He wanted to yank her to him and crush his mouth to hers, but instinct told him Ivy was a girl who appreciated a slow, steady seduction. So he took his time as long as his amped-up body would let him, nibbling at the corners of her mouth and coaxing her lips open with his tongue. The hand on her back rubbed small circles along her spine, and she folded into him, entangling her legs with his.

Her surrender shattered his control, and he rolled them over, pinning her to the bed. With one hand, he took her by the wrists and brought her arms up over her head so she could reach the headboard. "Grab on."

"Bossy, aren't we?" Her fists closed around the metal bars.

"Something like that." He reached over her to grab one of the condoms she'd deposited on the nightstand, ripped open the packet and rolled it on.

"I'm at your mercy." She flashed him a saucy smile and arched her back, thrusting her breasts up and inviting him to touch, taste and enjoy. "What now?"

"Now," he whispered against her lips, his breath mingling with hers, "we both get off."

Cade closed the slight distance between their mouths, and for the next few minutes there wasn't a lot of talking with the exception of a few "pleases," "mores" and "oh, Gods." She writhed under him, her lush softness rubbing against his impossibly hard cock. Christ, it felt like he could pound nails. Fortunately, he had a much more pleasant alternative in mind, one Ivy's frustrated movements said she was totally on board with.

He pried his mouth from hers. "Can't wait."

"Don't want you to." She tightened her grip on the headboard and spread her legs.

She was hot and wet and he was in her so fast he had to grit his teeth and run through the alarm codes to stop himself from coming immediately. Ten-one: call quarters. Ten-two: return to quarters. Ten-three: call dispatch...

"Cade," she moaned, snapping him out of his mental catalog.

"Say it again," he growled on another thrust.

"What?" She looked up at him, her eyes flaring, the pupils dark and shining.

"My name." He plunged into her again, slower, deeper, and he felt her muscles flutter and clench around him, sucking him in even further, holding him tighter. "I like how you say it when I'm inside you."

"Cade." She knotted her legs around his back, rolling her hips to meet each slick, steady stroke. "Please. I'm going to come."

"Do it." He pressed his lips to the sleek column of her neck, planting openmouthed kisses from her jaw to the cleft between her breasts. She tasted like she smelled, sweet and sunny. For a brief, terrifying moment he wondered if he'd ever get enough of her.

She shook her head, scattering her wild curls. "Not alone."

"You won't." He swiped a nipple with his tongue. Yep. Still sweet. Still sunny. Still not enough. "This time we go together."

"Need to touch you." She rattled the headboard, pleading with passion-filled eyes for him to give her permission to free her hands.

"Hell, yes," he hissed, sending a puff of air over her damp nipple. It sprang to attention, and he took it between his teeth, flicking it hard and fast with his tongue.

She released her grip on the bars and circled his neck, her nails digging into his shoulders, pressing him to her chest. "So good."

"Right there."

"Like that."

"I've got you." He raised himself up from his elbows to his palms, the muscles of his arms and back straining as he continued to move within her. "Let go."

"You, too." Ivy's voice came out on a tremble.

"God, yes." His was equally shaky.

As if his admission was a trigger, her body went taught, arcing beneath him as she cried out his name. He followed her into sweet oblivion, his release overwhelming him, rushing through him with the power of a back draft.

Ivy squeezed him tighter, her arms and legs holding him in a vise grip as he erupted. When he was finally spent, he rolled to his back, wrapping his arms around her and taking her with him.

He lay there in stunned silence, unable to speak, not knowing what to say if he could. The enormity of it came at him with the same force as his orgasm.

He'd just had the most raw, intense, soul-melting sex of his life.

With his best friend's sister.

And that fact left him with one burning question.

What now?

"Ivy."

Cade whispered her name again and shook her shoulder, but his efforts were met with silence. She nestled into him, her eyes closed, the curve of her red-brown lashes resting against her pale cheeks, her breathing deep and even.

Asleep.

He tried not to be offended. She must be exhausted, and not just from the mind-numbing sex. It wasn't every day she almost burned a house down and had to be rescued by the fire department.

His body relaxed and his arms curled protectively around her. There would be time enough for him to leave before morning. Right now she needed to sleep.

And he needed to figure out where the hell they went from here.

SUNLIGHT STREAMED THROUGH the window across Cade's face and chest. He raised an arm to shield his eyes and met something soft, warm and yielding.

Something that felt suspiciously like a female breast.

A smile played around the corners of his lips as memories of the night before came rushing back. Ivy under him, over him, gasping, breasts heaving, auburn curls splayed out around her like a halo. Calling his name when she came—twice—in a way that made his heart twist.

Then it hit him. Sunlight.

He'd stayed the night.

He never stayed the night.

He wasn't a complete jerk. He didn't fuck and run. He was all for a good postorgasm cuddle and maybe even round two after he'd had time to recover. But he made it a rule to be gone before sunrise. Less drama that way. Fewer expectations. And no chance of commitment. No chance he'd wind up in a relationship like his parents, so absorbed in each other—or their research—that they barely had time to acknowledge the world around them, including their own child.

But with Ivy he'd stayed for the cuddle, round two and the morning after. He should be panicked, jumping out of bed, grabbing his clothes and bolting for the door.

But he wasn't.

Instead, he was reaching for her again, the hand on her breast gently squeezing, his thumb brushing across her nipple.

What was wrong with him? Or was it that something was finally right?

"Mmm." Ivy stirred, rolling toward him and draping one leg over his thigh.

"You awake?" he asked, his breath stirring the hair at her temple.

"Must be dreaming," she murmured.

"No." He smiled against her cheek. "No dream. I'm right here. In the flesh."

He slid his mouth to hers and she shot upright, almost knocking him off the bed.

"What's wrong?" He raised himself up on his elbows and looked at her through eyes still heavy with sleep.

"I need to brush my teeth," she said, clapping a hand over her mouth and struggling to untangle herself from the sheets. "And my hair must look like a rat's nest."

"I like the way you look in the morning." Natural. Glowing. Satiated. His chest puffed with pride at the thought that he was responsible for the satiated part. "And it's not like I'm brushing my teeth, so don't sweat it."

He reached for her, but she rolled away.

"Two minutes." She stood, giving him a nice view of her very shapely, very naked ass as she crossed the room. "I'll be right back."

His eyes narrowed and his cock twitched with appreciation as he watched her retreating backside. He would've taken her for a wrap-herself-up-in-the-bedsheets kind of girl. He'd never been so glad to be wrong in his life.

"I'll be here."

The words felt strange but at the same time comfortable. Cade flopped down, arms crossed behind his head, to wait not-so-patiently. He was debating whether to go after her and get things started with a little shower action when the familiar, tinny strains of Nirvana's "Smells Like Teen Spirit" sounded from somewhere on the floor near the side of the bed.

He rolled over, reached down and fumbled for his pants. Pulling his cell out of the back pocket, he swiped the screen, not bothering to look at the display.

"Hardesty."

"Hey, man. You busy? I need a favor."

Gabe. Shit. So much for the shower.

"What's up?"

"I'm at my parents'. Devin and my mom are going over the wedding plans."

"And this concerns me how?"

"You gotta rescue me. If I hear the words *place setting*, *nosegay* or *fondant* one more time, I'm going to scream. I should have listened to Devin when she wanted to elope to Vegas. But I knew it'd break my mother's heart if her only son ran off and got married without her."

"You want me to come over there and kidnap you?"

"Nothing that drastic. Just meet me at Maude's for breakfast in ten. My treat."

Cade groaned inwardly. The last thing he wanted to do was break bread with the guy whose sister he'd just spent the better part of the last twelve hours screwing. But that guy was also his best friend, and the bro code dictated that friends always had each other's back. No exceptions.

Of course, the bro code also said you weren't supposed to bang your best friend's sister.

Looked like he was batting .500.

He threw off the sheet, sat up and groped for his boxers. "Make it thirty."

"Thirty it is," Gabe said, the relief in his voice coming through as clear as crystal. "Thanks, man."

Ivy came back just as Cade was shrugging on his

shirt. She'd tamed her hair—or tried to—and thrown on a robe, some of her modesty apparently returning in the harsh light of day. Her face fell at the sight of him almost fully dressed, making him feel like the biggest jerk on the face of the planet.

"You're leaving," she said simply.

He was tempted to lie and say it was work. But he'd never lied to her when they were friends, and he didn't want to lie to her now that they were…whatever they were. "Yeah, sorry. I got this call…"

She waved him off. "You don't have to explain. I knew what this was going in."

"That makes one of us." He dropped the sneaker in his hand and sat on the bed, his mission to bail out Gabe momentarily forgotten. "Tell me, what exactly do you think happened here last night?"

She went to the closet and rummaged through it, tossing aside clothes as she went. "We scratched an itch."

Her voice was light and her movements casual, but he wasn't buying it. He'd known her too long and too well to miss the signs. The too-broad smile trying unsuccessfully to hide the shadow behind her eyes.

She was hurting. And he was the one who'd hurt her.

Fuck.

"Ivy."

A little black dress flew over her shoulder. He squeezed his eyes shut, fighting the image of it hugging her curves.

"Ivy."

The dress was joined by a skirt.

Cade came up behind her, spun her around and plucked a blouse out of her hands. "Stop."

"I told you, you don't have to explain. I get it. We had our fun, but now it's done."

"Says who?"

"Huh?"

"Who says our fun has to be done?" He tossed the blouse onto the bed and reached out to cup her cheek, rubbing his thumb along her jawline. "What if I get another itch?"

She shrugged off his hand. "I'm sure you'll find someone else to scratch it."

"What if it's an itch only you can scratch?"

"Stop messing with me." She took a step back, and he followed, keeping her close.

"I'm not messing with you." Cade put his hands on her hips, drawing her to him. "Look, I know you're only here on loan. And pretty soon you'll be back to your fabulous, jet-setting life. But we're both adults, right? Why not enjoy each other while we can?"

Ivy bit her lip, hesitating, and for an agonizing minute Cade wondered if he'd made a colossal mistake. Then she relaxed against him, and he breathed a relieved sigh.

"You mean you want to keep doing...whatever it is we're doing?"

"Hell, yeah." He grinned. It was damned adorable how she couldn't quite bring herself to put a name to their extracurricular activities. "Don't you?"

"Won't it get...weird?"

"Not if we don't let it," he insisted. "And we won't."

"Now I'm confused." She shook her head, her curls spilling around her shoulders. "If you're not running from me, then why are you running?"

"I'm not."

She started to protest, but he stopped her with a quick,

hard kiss. "At least not voluntarily. Your brother called and asked me to meet him at Maude's. Devin and your mom are talking shoes and rice, and he needed a break. I couldn't very well tell him I'd rather spend the day in bed with his sister."

"Hmm." She nodded thoughtfully, one side of her mouth curling into a half smile. "I see your problem."

"How about a do-over?" The hands on her hips tightened, pulling her flush against him. "Like maybe tonight?"

"A do-over?" She smirked. "What are we, back in middle school?"

"What I've got planned is way beyond the limits of my impressionable, prepubescent mind."

"God, you're incorrigible."

"And by incorrigible you mean irresistible, right?" He waggled his brows at her.

"Yes, damn you." She gave him a little push. "Go. Have breakfast with my brother. I should get to the nursery anyway. If someone's not watching Dad, he'll probably do something crazy, like try to move twenty cubic yards of mulch by himself."

"So we're good?" Cade asked, releasing her.

"We're good." Ivy started for her closet again but stopped after a couple of steps and turned back to him, the tiny creases in her forehead telling him something was still bothering her. He didn't have to wait long to find out what it was. "We're going to keep this between us, right? The last thing I need is my family thinking we're an item."

"Fine by me. I'm not sure I'd be able to look Gabe in the eye if he knew we'd been…" Cade scratched his chin, grasping for a more Ivy-friendly phrase than "doing the nasty." Bumping uglies? Getting it on? "…intimate. Never mind your father."

"So we're agreed. We keep things quiet and casual."

"Quiet and casual," he repeated, sitting on the bed again and reaching for the sneaker he'd discarded.

Just what he needed after the mess with Sasha.

He hoped.

8

"MY GOD, IVY." Hank, the photographer Ivy had been filling in for, sat hunched over her laptop, clicking through
the photos from the calendar shoot. "These are incred-
ible."

"Thanks." She stood behind him and looked over his
shoulder, shifting her weight from one foot to the other.
"I had good material to work with."

"I'll grant you that." He paused, his finger hovering
over the mouse, a picture of a smiling Cade with Bilbo
perched on his shoulder frozen on the screen. "But this
is more than good material. This is good photography."

"Again, thanks." Ivy dragged her eyes away from
Cade's seminude image, her face heating with the memories of their sex-capades the night before. And the
night before that. And the night before that.

Did Hank have to stop on that photo?

Mercifully, he clicked on to the next one before she
started drooling.

"It's me who should be thanking you for bailing me
out." He clicked again, pausing to take a sip of coffee
from a mug that looked like it hadn't seen the inside of

a dishwasher in years. "You know, you don't need me for this. You could have picked the final proofs yourself. I trust your judgment, and I'm sure the shelter board does, too."

"I didn't want to step on any toes. The calendar is still your project. You started it. I figured you should finish it, now that your back's feeling better."

"It's getting there." He sat up straight and stretched to one side and then the other. "But it's not one hundred percent. Doctor's got me on restricted activity."

"What about your business?" She glanced around Hank's cluttered studio, noticing for the first time the thin layer of dust on the equipment.

"See that pile of papers?" He gestured to a stack next to the cordless phone. "All clients I have to call and break the news that I'm out of commission for the time being."

Ivy pulled a chair up next to him and sat, her mind spinning with half-formed ideas. "What kinds of clients?"

"The usual. Weddings, engagement photos, birthdays. A couple of family portraits. And one woman who wants me to take glamour shots of her cats." A muscle ticked in his jaw. "Florian's going to shit himself."

"Who's Florian?"

"Florian Rhodes. The only other professional photographer in town. Total hack, if you ask me. He usually gets my overflow business." Hank took another sip from his ancient mug and grimaced, whether because of the coffee or the competition, Ivy didn't know. "What the hell kind of name is Florian, anyway? I bet he made it up. He looks more like a Jake to me. Or maybe a James. I had an assistant named James once. Real pain in the ass. Refused to answer to Jim. He quit before I could fire him."

"What if I cover for you for the next few weeks?" Ivy scooted to the edge of her chair. "Like I did with the calendar."

"Why would you want to do that?" He scratched at his temple. "I mean, the calendar was for charity. But bar mitzvahs? Pet portraits? You're used to working with professionals, not local yokels."

She shrugged. "It'll be a nice change. Except for the pet-portrait thing. I'm not touching that."

"Can't say I blame you. Might as well stick Florian with that one." He grabbed the papers and handed them to her. "Here. Have at it. You might recognize a few of the names. Anything you book, we split fifty-fifty. Deal?"

"Deal." She flipped through the stack. Hank was right. She did recognize a few of the names. More than a few. Earl Gibson, owner of the local grocery store, was looking for someone to photograph a surprise birthday party he was throwing for his wife. Maude wanted some new publicity shots for the diner. Even Jessie Pagano, who'd tortured Holly all through high school, needed a photographer for her son's preschool graduation.

Okay, so maybe she'd pass that last one on to Florian, too.

Like Hank had said, the others were more of the same. Special occasions. Family reunions. Definitely not her typical fare. But the more she leafed through the pile, the more the idea appealed to her—capturing regular, everyday people at the happiest times of their lives, instead of moody models primped to the nines and posed for the camera.

What the heck? She'd be in Stockton for at least a few more weeks. She was usually done at the nursery by noon. She needed something to occupy the rest of her days besides counting down the hours until her next round between the sheets with Cade.

"I think I'll start with this one." She held up a slip of paper. "The mayor needs a new head shot."

"Good choice." Hank nodded. "I did her back when she was on the board of selectmen. She's easy to work with."

Ivy rolled her eyes. "No one can be more difficult than a food-and-sleep-deprived swimsuit model forced to stand in forty-degree water to midthigh and keep her balance against strong waves and heavy wind."

"You'd be surprised." He pushed his chair back, pulled out the top drawer of his desk and hunted through the contents until he pulled out a key. "I suppose if we're going to be working together you ought to have this. Then you can come and go as you please."

"Thanks." She took the key from him and slipped it into her pocket, making a mental note to add it to her key chain later. "You can trust me."

"I wouldn't have given you free rein if I didn't." He handed her the phone. "I'm going to head home, take some Motrin and fire up the heating pad. Let me know how you make out. And lock up when you're done."

With an awkward wave, he left. Ivy stood and surveyed the room. They'd rented a bigger space for the calendar shoot. Hank's studio was small and somewhat cramped, but it had all the equipment she needed for indoor shots. Studio strobes. Light diffusers. Umbrellas. Reflectors. Tripods.

And of course she had her own trusty Nikon and enough lenses to cover pretty much every perspective, from wide angle to close up.

She ran a finger over one of the strobes. It came back covered in grime. She'd have to find where Hank kept his cleaning supplies and give the place a good going-over before she could even think about bringing clients in.

But first she had some phone calls to make.

CADE MOVED QUICKLY and efficiently through his locker, checking his gear. His turnout was ready to go, his helmet, flashlight and the face piece for his breathing apparatus all in place. He replaced the battery in his radio, making sure it was set on the dispatch channel, and went to the engine bay to check the rest of his breathing unit on the rig.

"Hardesty." O'Brien, the engineer, stuck his head out of the driver's window. "Nice of you to join us."

"Us?" Cade looked around the engine bay. "You got multiple personalities or something? Because I don't see anyone else in here."

"Sykes and Hansen are restocking the ambulance. Guess C Company had a rough day. Three MVAs, a couple of miscellaneous medical calls and a structure fire."

"Any fatalities?" Cade held his breath for the answer. In a suburb the size of Stockton, he was bound to know the victims, or at least know somebody who knew them. It was like that six-degrees-of-separation thing, only closer.

"No." Even O'Brien had the decency to look relieved. Maybe he had a heart under his asshole exterior after all. "Just some minor injuries. Nothing life-threatening."

"Well, let's hope it's a quiet night."

Then maybe he could head over to Ivy's after his shift. Had it only been a week since he'd showed up on her doorstep with his version of a fire safety kit? How was it that in that short time she'd become as essential to him as breathing?

"You got plans with your girlfriend? Presuming, of course, she doesn't get her fat ass stuck in any more tight places."

So much for the heart theory. The guy was not only a prick, he was a mind reader. Dangerous combination.

Cade ignored him and concentrated on prechecking his gear. As much as he wanted to pound O'Brien into next week, he wasn't stupid enough to get caught fighting on duty and risk an automatic suspension.

"O'Brien." Cappy's voice came over the loudspeaker. "Report to my office. Stat."

Cade gave a long, low whistle. "Someone's in trouble."

"Or due for a promotion." O'Brien jumped down from the cab and leaned against the side of the engine. "I took the lieutenant exam last month. Results must be in."

He sneered at Cade, who was trying his hardest to focus on testing his regulator. "Looks like I'm going to be your superior, Hardesty. Think you can stomach calling me 'sir'?"

"When hell freezes over."

"When hell freezes over, sir," O'Brien mocked over his shoulder as he strode out of the engine bay.

Cade shook his head and continued his preshift ritual. He'd transfer to another station before he'd work under O'Brien. Or maybe take the lieutenant exam himself. It was past time—way past time, if he was honest with himself. Cappy had been bugging him to take it for years. But Cade had always put it off, claiming he was too busy or too tired or just happy doing what he was doing and didn't want the extra responsibility.

Bullshit.

Truth was, he was too damn scared of failing.

He'd made it through high school thanks to Gabe and Ivy, who'd tutored him in every subject from physics to precalculus. College had been a haze of football and frat parties, and he'd passed the firefighters exam by the narrowest of margins. On his second try.

No wonder he was such a disappointment to his academic parents. Mom with her books on French romantic poetry and Dad with his encyclopedic knowledge of the flora and fauna of North America. They'd both been tenured professors at Wesleyan before their "retirement" to North Carolina's research triangle. Never mind that they worked as much now between adjunct teaching, book signings and speaking engagements as they did then.

But he wasn't stupid, no matter what his parents thought. He'd aced the practical-skills part of his firefighter training. He just froze when it came to taking tests. The words seemed to swim across the page, and the more nervous he got, the worse it got. After talking with Nick, who'd gone public with his dyslexia, Cade had started to wonder if he might have a learning disability, too. And he'd never gotten the help he needed because his parents had been too preoccupied—or too proud—to notice.

But the Nelsons had always been there for him. Especially Gabe and Ivy. Maybe she'd help him study now, if she wasn't off photographing supermodels in some exotic locale by the time the test rolled around again.

"Hey, Cade." Sykes strolled into the engine bay, his constant companion Hansen at his heels, their arms filled with medical supplies. "Up for a cutthroat game of Uno after dinner?"

"Sure." With one last glance at his gear, Cade closed the doors of the equipment compartment and turned his attention to the paramedics. He didn't think he'd ever been so glad to see those two clowns in his life. Anything to keep his mind off Ivy and her inevitable departure.

"Need any help?" he asked. If Yin and Yang weren't enough of a distraction, maybe stocking meds would do the trick.

"Nah." Hansen swung open the rear doors of the ambulance. "We got it covered."

"Then I think I'll squeeze in a workout before dinner." Cade pushed his shoulders back and rolled his neck. "Who's cooking?"

"Cappy." Sykes grimaced and climbed on board after his partner.

"I'll chip in for pizza." Hansen stuck his head out of the vehicle and waved a bill at Cade.

"Me, too." Sykes followed suit.

"I'm in." Cade collected the money and stuck it in his pocket. "Bacon and onion okay?"

"Fine by me." Hansen disappeared back inside the rig.

"Me, too." Sykes pulled another bill out of his wallet and handed it to Cade. "And get me a sausage-and-spinach calzone for later."

Cade shook his head. The guy was a bottomless pit. How he stayed within the on-duty weight limit was a mystery. "No problem. I'll call Valentino's when I'm done working out."

"Thanks, man."

Sykes vanished after his partner, and Cade headed

for the fitness room. He hadn't gone two feet when the alarm sounded and Cappy's voice boomed over the speaker again.

"Engine Five, Rescue One. Ten thirty-seven, Code two. Victim trapped in a drainage pipe at 71 East Main Street."

Cade sprinted for his locker. Heavy footsteps told him Sykes and Hansen were close behind. They met O'Brien and Cappy and the rest of B Company, who were already pulling on their turnouts.

"71 East Main Street. Isn't that the Bag 'n' Feed?" Sykes asked.

Cade toed off his sneakers and stepped into his bunker pants. "How the hell does a person get stuck in the drain pipe at a convenience store?"

"It's not a person," Cappy informed him. "It's a cat. Employees said they heard it in there a couple of days ago. They hoped it would work its way out, but no dice."

"We're dispatching an engine and an ambulance to rescue a fucking cat?" O'Brien stopped with one suspender hanging off his shoulder.

Cappy glared at him. "You got something better to do?"

O'Brien silently threaded his arm through the suspender into his gear.

"Anyone else got any complaints?" Cappy looked from man to man, his expression daring someone else to object.

"No, Cap," they chimed.

"Good." Cappy slammed his locker shut and jammed on his helmet. "Then let's get moving. There's a feline life at stake. And contrary to popular opinion, they don't have nine."

9

"ARE YOU SURE you're okay?" Noelle stared at her sister across the kitchen table.

"That's like the tenth time you've asked me that." Ivy stabbed an asparagus spear with her fork. "And for the tenth time, I'm fine. You didn't have to drive all the way up here to check on me. Unannounced."

Thank goodness Cade was on duty tonight, although she was pretty sure he planned on swinging by after his shift. She'd texted him to keep right on going if he saw Noelle's MINI Cooper in the driveway.

"Yeah, I kind of did." Noelle looked at her own, barely touched plate of food as if the grilled chicken, brown rice and mixed vegetables were her mortal enemies. "Mom made me promise."

"Mom?" Ivy froze, her fork halfway to her mouth.

Noelle cut off the teeny tiniest bit of chicken and nibbled at it. "She said you'd been acting strange lately. Forgetting stuff at the nursery. Mixing up deliveries. Ordering the wrong seeds."

It figured their mother was involved. Nothing got past her. Especially not the way Ivy had been walking around with her head in the clouds for the past week. Not that she was admitting that to Noelle.

"Honest mistakes. I haven't worked the sales floor in years. A lot has changed. It takes a little getting used to." Ivy bit off the top of the asparagus spear. "Anyway, I hired a part-timer to cover afternoons and weekends, so I can concentrate on opening in the mornings and doing the books. And keep up with Hank's slack."

She'd done her first gig, the mayor's publicity shots, the day after Hank had handed over his contacts. It had gone great, as had the other jobs she'd covered that week: a family portrait, a sweet sixteen and a ribbon-cutting ceremony at the local hospital.

What she'd told Hank had proved right ten times over. It was a lot more fun—and rewarding—taking photos of normal, happy people doing normal, happy stuff. Sure, it was still hard work, running around, bending, crouching, contorting herself into all sorts of strange positions to get the right camera or lighting angle. And yeah, there was plenty of drama at the sweet sixteen with something like fifty girls fighting over the handful of boys in attendance. But it was nothing compared to the hissy fit one model threw when she was served the wrong brand of mineral water. Or the time a *Sports Illustrated* cover girl walked off set just because Ivy asked her to remove her belly-button ring.

"An extra pair of hands is nice, and it's sweet that you're helping Hank," Noelle said, cutting into Ivy's thoughts. "But that's all beside the point."

"And what is the point, exactly?"

"The point is you're distracted." Noelle paused for dramatic effect, using the time to eat a few grains of rice. "Mom thinks you're seeing someone."

Ivy almost choked on her chicken. "Aside from the people at the nursery and my photography clients, the insides of my eyelids when I fall into bed at the end of the day are about all I'm seeing."

"You know what I mean." Noelle put her fork down and tented her hands under her chin. "She thinks you're hot and heavy with some guy."

"Mom's words?"

"Close enough."

"Has she checked out the available dating pool in this town? There's not exactly a bumper crop of eligible males."

"That's what I told her." Noelle drummed her fingers together. "But she's pretty insistent. Says she knows when one of her *bambini* is ready to take the plunge."

"The plunge?"

"Fall in love." Noelle let a wistful half smile creep onto her face, and Ivy wondered if she wasn't the only one hiding something. "All Mom's words this time."

"Then why isn't she having this conversation with me?"

"She figured you'd talk more freely to your baby sister."

"She figured wrong." Ivy stood and started to clear the table. "Want some coffee? I won't bother to ask about dessert."

"Nice change of subject, but you're not getting out of this that easy." Noelle fished something out of her Birkin bag and held it up between her fingertips. "And I brought my own herbal tea."

"Why am I not surprised?" Ivy grabbed the kettle off the stove and filled it with water.

"My trainer says it cleanses my system and supports

my body's natural defenses." Noelle sat back in her chair and crossed her long, dancer's legs, clearly settling in for the long haul. "But back to you and your mystery man."

"There is no mystery man." Ivy clanged the kettle back down on the stove and turned on the burner.

"Mom says otherwise. And her romance radar is never wrong. She called it with Holly and Nick. She even pegged Gabe and Devin, and no one saw that coming."

"Well, she's wrong this time." Ivy picked up the remote for the thirteen-inch, flat-screen TV mounted under the cabinet by the sink. "Mind if I turn on the news? They're doing a piece on the mayor's new community parks initiative, and they're going to use the head shot I took for her."

She hit the power button and flicked to the local news channel, but instead of the mayor the screen showed a group of rescue workers huddled around a hole in what looked like the parking lot of the Bag 'n' Feed. Then the screen flashed and the picture changed to a shot of one of the workers being carried off on a stretcher.

It was a worker in turnout gear with a familiar head of dirty blond hair, now matted to his forehead, and blue eyes, usually dancing with mischief, hard and flat with pain.

"Hey." Noelle stood and came up behind Ivy for a closer look at the TV. "Isn't that Cade? Turn up the volume."

Ivy didn't—couldn't—move.

Noelle snatched the remote from her and pumped up the volume several levels.

"A seemingly innocuous rescue turned dangerous today at the Bag 'n' Feed on East Main Street. Crews were working to free a kitten from a drainage pipe outside the store when a firefighter was struck by a drunk driver. Onlookers say the firefighter was injured when he pushed several bystanders out of the car's path. No names have been released, but sources say both the driver and the firefighter were taken to St. Raphael's Hospital for treatment. The cat was eventually freed and is recuperating at the Stockton Animal Clinic, which has already received a number of adoption requests."

"Who cares about the cat?" Ivy screamed at the television. "What about Cade?"

"So that *was* him." Noelle grabbed the cordless phone off the counter.

"What are you doing?" Ivy asked, her voice rising several notches to a pitch she was pretty sure only dogs could hear. How could her sister stay so calm with Cade hurt, maybe seriously?

"Calling the hospital. Hopefully they can tell us something about Cade's condition."

"Screw that. I'm going over there." Ivy pushed past her sister, turned off the stove and hunted for her purse. Where had she left the damned thing? She could have sworn she'd seen it somewhere.

"Oh. My. God. Mom was right." Noelle followed Ivy into the living room. "There is a guy. Cade."

"We're friends. That's all." Ivy found her bag behind the couch and fished out her keys.

"Give me a little credit, Ivy." Noelle tossed the cordless phone onto the sofa. "You've had a thing for him since you were in diapers. Who could blame you for finally making your move?"

"Look, I don't have time to argue with you about this now. Are you coming with me or not?"

"Oh, I'm coming with you, all right." Noelle plucked Ivy's keys out of her hand. "In fact, I'm driving."

"Then we're taking your car." Ivy snatched the keys back and dropped them into her purse. "It's faster."

CADE TURNED HIS head at the *whoosh* of his hospital room door. A nurse in pink scrubs strode through, followed by Cappy, Sykes and Hansen, still in their turnouts, their faces streaked with dirt and worry.

"Two minutes," the nurse admonished them, hands on her hips for emphasis. "That's it. He's heavily medicated and he needs rest."

"Yes, ma'am," Cappy answered for the rest of the crew.

The nurse gave him a curt nod and left.

"How's the cat?" Cade tried to smile, but his face felt numb.

"A damn sight better than you," Sykes joked, moving into the room to Cade's bedside.

"And before you ask, the two bystanders you saved are fine, too," Hansen added, joining his partner.

"Thank God," Cade croaked, his throat dry.

"They want to thank you." Cappy stopped at the foot of the bed. "The department's already talking about an awards ceremony."

"I was just doing my job." A job he wouldn't be doing for the next six weeks, minimum, Cade thought, grimacing at the cast on his left leg.

"You know how the brass is." Cappy sighed. "Always willing to cash in on a chance for some publicity."

"The press will eat you up with those movie-star good looks," Sykes teased.

Hansen nodded. "They're camped outside, waiting for you to be released."

"Well, they're going to be waiting a while. We're keeping him overnight for observation." The nurse was back with a cup of water and some pills. She handed both to Cade. "Take these. They'll help you sleep."

With a groan, he propped himself up, popped the pills into his mouth and washed them down. "Thanks."

Then he collapsed against the pillow.

The nurse checked the chart hanging by the bed and turned to Cade's guests. "Time for you boys to leave. I broke protocol to get you in here after visiting hours, but that's only because I've got a soft spot for first responders."

"No problem, ma'am," Cappy said.

"Call me *ma'am* again and there'll be a problem." The nurse's smile softened her snappy rejoinder.

"We'll see you tomorrow, Cade." Hansen gave the blanket an awkward pat.

"Let us know if you need anything." Sykes clapped Cade on the shoulder. "Like booze. Or broads. Or dirty magazines."

"Very funny. Now get out of here and let me sleep."

Cade closed his eyes and listened until the only sounds were the beeps and whirs of the monitors.

His head ached. His leg throbbed. Broken in two places, the doctors said. They also said he was lucky it wasn't worse. Both clean breaks, no need for surgery. No internal bleeding, all his vital organs intact.

But he didn't feel lucky. He felt like shit.

Six weeks in a cast meant six weeks out of work. Maybe longer until he got cleared for more than light duty.

What the hell was he supposed to do until then? He

lived the job. He was the job. His days and nights, work and free time, all revolved around the station.

Fucking pathetic.

It was no surprise that the guys from B Company had been his only visitors. His own parents hadn't even called. The hospital had left a message for them as his next of kin, but as far as he knew they hadn't bothered to respond. And Ivy...

Ivy.

Did she even know he was hurt? It wasn't like he could ask the nurses to call her, with their relationship a better-kept secret than the formula for Coca-Cola. And he didn't have a clue what had happened to his cell phone.

He reached for the nightstand and fumbled around. No phone, but he did manage to knock over a plastic pitcher of water and the TV remote.

Cade sank back onto the pillow. His eyes drifted shut again and his breathing slowed. Whatever the doctor had given him was working, that was for sure. And that meant whatever he wanted to say to Ivy would have to wait for morning.

Until then, he'd have to be satisfied with dreaming about her.

It could have been ten minutes or ten hours later when soft voices pierced his semicomatose state.

"Are you sure this is okay?"

Ivy?

"Sure, I'm sure."

The pink-scrubbed nurse.

"I don't want to get you in any trouble."

Yep. Definitely Ivy.

"Don't worry, it'll be fine. If anyone asks, just tell them you're his fiancée."

His what?

"His…what?" Ivy said, echoing his thoughts.

"Fiancée. They won't bother you then."

"Okay. Thanks."

"My pleasure. The pictures you took at the ribbon cutting for the new pediatric ER were great. My supervisor loved them."

Rubber soles squeaked, the door *whooshed* and the scrape of wood on the linoleum floor told Cade the nurse had left and Ivy had pulled up a chair next to his bed. Her hand rested lightly on his arm just above his IV, and the sunny, springy scent he'd come to associate with her mixed with the pungent, antiseptic smells of the hospital.

He cracked open one eye slowly, hesitantly, afraid to find out he might still be dreaming.

"Hey." *Nope. Not a dream.* The hand on his arm trembled along with her voice. "You're awake."

He opened both eyes, blinking against the glare of the hospital's harsh fluorescent lights. "You're here."

"Is that…okay?"

"Of course it's okay." He gave her a weak smile that he hoped she read as reassuring and not *scary clown*. "It's better than okay."

"I heard some of the guys from the station came by."

"Yeah." He cleared his throat and struggled to sit up. "My parents…"

"I spoke to them." She cut him off. "They're in Edmonton. You dad's giving the keynote at a botany conference and your mom's working on a paper she's coauthoring with a professor at King's University College. They wanted to know if they should cut their trip short and fly down."

"God, no." His stomach rolled at the thought. He'd never hear the end of it if his little accident interrupted their precious careers.

"That's what I told them, after I reassured them your condition wasn't life threatening."

"Thanks."

"They're idiots." She squeezed his hand.

"I know." He squeezed back. She got him. She really got him. Anyone else would spout some crap about how his parents loved him in their own way. Not Ivy. She knew better. And so did he. He was barely a blip on their radar, an afterthought in their busy lives. On the rare occasions when they did remember his existence, it was to rehash what an embarrassment he was to them. His lack of ambition. His blue-collar job. His parade of women.

He half closed his eyes and let his head fall back. It was starting to pound again, no doubt thanks to his parents and the lighting.

Ivy released his hand and stood. "You're tired. I should go."

"Stay." He reached out to her, eyes fully open now. "Please."

She shuffled her feet and tugged on the hem of her shirt. "What will people say?"

"What people?"

"It's a small town. People talk."

"So don't listen." He ignored the pounding in his head and stared at her, his eyes starting to water but his gaze unmoving.

She hesitated for a second before reclaiming her seat and his hand. "Okay. Until you're asleep."

He closed his eyes and let out his breath on a long, slow, pain-infused sigh. "Good enough."

For now.

10

WHEN CADE WOKE up the next morning, Ivy was still there, sprawled in the chair, head back, mouth open, snoring adorably.

The corners of Cade's mouth curled into a smile. Who knew snoring could be cute?

"I see one of you is awake." A nurse, this one in lime green, came in with a tray of brown-and-gray institutional food. She wheeled a table over the bed, set the tray on it and pressed a button on the bed rail to raise the head until he was almost in a sitting position. "Eat up. You're being released. The doctor will be by in a few minutes with your discharge papers."

"Great." Six weeks of daytime talk shows and bad reality TV. Maybe he could convince Cappy to let him come in a couple of hours a day and do paperwork or something.

Ivy sat up and yawned, revealing a strip of creamy white skin between her waistband and the bottom of her shirt. "I'll make sure he follows doctor's orders and takes it easy."

What was she, a mind reader?

He reached down to adjust the blanket. His leg might be immobilized, but other parts down under were working just fine.

"I have a feeling that's going to be a challenge." The nurse smiled at Ivy then turned back to Cade. "I'll go get the doctor and your morning meds."

"I can hardly wait."

"Don't be such a grump," Ivy said as the nurse left. "You're getting sprung from this place. You should be happy."

"Yeah, happy." He picked up his fork and pushed around a pile of goop that he suspected was some sort of potato. "I'll get to catch up on Jerry Springer. Learn to play the guitar. Reach level one hundred in *Candy Crush Saga*."

"You could always study for the lieutenant exam."

He froze with the fork halfway to his mouth. "How do you know about that?"

"I saw the books in the backseat of your SUV." She rolled her neck one way and then the other. "When is the test?"

"Cappy gave those to me." Cade shoveled in a forkful of gooey potato and grimaced. They tasted more like the dirt they were grown in than any spud he'd ever encountered. "I'm not even registered."

"So get registered."

"You might have left Stockton in the rearview mirror and forgotten half of high school, but I haven't." He peeled back the lid on a plastic cup of orange juice, needing something to rid his taste buds of the sticky residue of the potatoes. "Test taking isn't exactly my strong suit. I wouldn't have graduated high school if it wasn't for you and Gabe pulling me through."

"I haven't forgotten Stockton. Or you." She lowered her head, but not before he saw the mist in her eyes. "And who's to say we won't pull you through again? You said it yourself, Cade. We're friends. We'll always be friends. And friends look out for each other."

She stood, stretched and disappeared into the bathroom.

Cade scowled at his plate. Now she was the one throwing the *F* word around. And he was the one who didn't like it one damn bit, something he didn't want to analyze too closely.

Talk about ironic. Alanis Morissette had nothing on him.

"Holy crap." Ivy's voice drifted through the open door. "Why didn't you tell me I looked like Ursula the Sea Witch? My hair's all over the place."

"I've always thought Ursula was kind of hot." He sipped his juice, grateful for the change of subject. "She's got a great rack. So do you."

"Thanks for noticing." She popped her head out the door. She'd tried to tamp down her curls with water, but all she'd succeeded in doing was creating a hotter, wetter mess. "You must be on the mend if you're ogling my breasts."

"Honey, I've been ogling them since the calendar shoot. There just wasn't a polite time to mention it until now."

He winked at her, and she ducked back into the bathroom. He downed the rest of his juice, pretty much the only edible thing on the tray. He was even a little afraid to try the coffee.

"How's our patient doing this morning?" The doctor picked that moment to not-so-conveniently interrupt, bursting through the door with the nurse trailing behind him. He plucked Cade's chart from a hook next to the bed and flipped through it. "Ready to go home?"

"You bet." Cade tried to hoist himself up and was rewarded with a blinding bolt of pain that shot from his knee to his ankle.

"Good." The doctor handed the chart to the nurse, pulled a pad from the pocket of his lab coat and started scribbling. "I'm writing you two prescriptions, a painkiller and an antibiotic. No baths or showers for the next two days. Then you can clean yourself up, but cover your cast with a plastic bag and seal it to keep out any moisture. Elevate the leg whenever you can, and don't be afraid to ice it if it starts to swell. Diane will get you some crutches, but I'd prefer that you stay off your feet as much as possible. And if your bedroom's on the second floor, you'll want to set up something downstairs until the cast comes off."

Cade swore under his breath. "That's gonna be a problem. My apartment's on the second floor of a two-family house."

The doctor put the prescriptions on the bed table and stuck his pad back in his pocket. "Is there somewhere else you can stay while you're recuperating?"

Cade shook his head. "I don't think…"

"He can stay with me." Ivy came out of the bathroom, her hair a little tamer. "There's a guest room on the first floor. It's perfect."

Perfect? More like letting the fox in the henhouse. Not that the fox was complaining.

"Ivy, you don't have to—"

She cut him off with a wave of her hand. "I know I don't. I want to. Besides, what choice do you have?"

She had a good point. He didn't really have any other options with his parents AWOL, Gabe in the city and his buddy Trey's place in worse shape than his own.

"Then it's settled. As soon as Diane goes through the rest of your discharge instructions and makes you a follow-up appointment, she'll release you to your girl-friend's care." The doctor extended his hand, and Cade shook it. "Good luck, Mr. Hardesty. We'll see you in a few weeks."

He left the room, followed by the nurse, who stopped and turned at the door. "I'll be right back with a pair of crutches, your valuables and some information from the nutritionist."

The door swung shut behind her, leaving Cade alone with Ivy.

"I'll be in this thing for six weeks." He sat up, swung his good leg over the side of the bed and thumped his cast with his fist. Bad idea. Pain radiated down his leg. He did his best to ignore it and plowed on. "Will you even be here that long?"

"My dad's nowhere near ready to go back to work full-time." Ivy sat next to him on the bed, giving the cast a wide berth. "And I promised the shelter I'd be here for their benefit on Labor Day weekend when they unveil the calendar."

"We'd be living together." He eyed her, remembering her words from the night before. "What will people say?"

"I thought you weren't worried about small-town gossip."

"I thought you were."

She gave a halfhearted shrug. "We're friends, remember? Friends help each other. No one has to know any more than that."

There she went with the *F* word again. But even that wasn't enough to stop Cade's heart from doing a celebratory jig. Six weeks under the same roof as Ivy. Suddenly his forced incapacitation didn't seem so much like a prison sentence. It'd be like old times, when he, Ivy and Gabe had spent hours hanging out in the Nelsons' basement, watching TV and playing video games.

Except minus Gabe. And swap out the video games for screwing like rabbits.

"I can be pretty demanding," Cade warned.

"I can handle demanding."

"How about sponge baths?" He leaned in to her, barely resisting the impulse to bury his face in her hair, sexily mussed from a night of sleeping in a hospital chair. "Can you handle those?"

"Sponge baths?"

"You heard the doctor. No baths or showers."

"For two days." She playfully pushed his shoulder. "Not six weeks."

He pushed back. "You can't blame a guy for trying."

"Um, do you have any clothes?" She craned her neck to catch a glimpse of his exposed back. "As attractive as that hospital gown is, I don't think you want to walk down the hall with your backside hanging out."

"Check the closet when you're done checking out my ass. I think they put the stuff I was wearing under my turnouts in there."

She went to the closet and opened the door. "Nope. Nothing."

"Could you run by my place and grab me a pair of gym shorts and a T-shirt?"

"What about underwear?"

"Optional." He fell back onto the pillow, crossing his arms behind his head.

She rolled her eyes. "I'll take that as a yes."

"You just want to get your hands on my skivvies." He grinned. "Again."

"Aw, shucks." She grinned back. "You got me."

"You'll have to swing by the station first. I left my keys there."

"No problem." She scooped up her purse from the floor and fished out her cell phone. "I'll call someone to come get me. I'm sure Noelle's long gone by now."

"Hey, roomie." His voice made her stop rummaging and look up. "One more favor."

"Name it."

"If you're going to rifle through my delicates, I'm partial to the bright blue ones with Pac-Man on the crotch."

"HERE WE ARE." Ivy fumbled with the key, her hands damp and shaky. After a few tries, she managed to get it into the lock and let them in. "Home, sweet temporary home."

"Thanks." Cade planted his crutches and maneuvered his way into the entryway with more ease than Ivy could have managed if she'd have been using the darned things for half a century.

She picked up the duffel bag she'd stuffed with clothes when she stopped at Cade's apartment and followed him inside. "Let's get you settled on the couch in the living room. I'll show you your room later."

"I'm not a cripple." He looked down at his plaster-encased leg and frowned. "Well, I am, but I can hobble a few steps to the couch under my own power."

"Stubborn man."

"Persistent woman."

"I guess we'll have to agree to disagree." She dropped the duffel in the foyer and continued to follow him into the living room, smiling at his back as they went. "My house, my rules."

He lowered himself onto the sofa and laid his crutches on the floor. "Do your rules include doing the deed? Or at least some heavy petting? Because I'm feeling kind of lonely down here. And horny."

"The doctor said you should rest."

"My leg. Not my…"

"Slow down, sailor." She gently lifted his foot and propped a pillow under it. "We've got plenty of time for that. You're stuck with me for the foreseeable future."

"I don't consider it being stuck." He caught her hand before she could move away. "And as my private-duty nurse, I should think you'd want to tend to my welfare."

"Am I going to have to get you one of those annoying bells so you can summon me at will?" She tried to pull away, but he held fast, his thumb tracing figure eights on her palm.

"That's not a bad idea. Or I can always yodel."

"You yodel?" She gave in to the strange magnetism he seemed to assert over her and sat gingerly beside his prone form.

"I'll learn."

"I should warn you. I'm not the nurturing type."

His hand snaked up and around to the back of her head, his fingers curling into her hair and drawing her down to him. "It's not nurturing I'm looking for, sweetheart."

"We can't."

His lips touched hers, and her breath hitched. "We can."

"Then we shouldn't." She flattened her palms against his chest, intending to push him away but instead finding herself clutching his T-shirt. Heat scorched her hands through the soft cotton and she could feel his heartbeat under the hard muscles of his chest.

"Yes." His lips brushed hers, and hot little shivers ran up and down her spine. "We should."

"I'll hurt you." She glanced at his leg, stretched out on the couch behind her.

He cupped her cheek and turned her face back to him, bringing them so close his mouth was at her ear, his breath warm on her skin. "No, you won't."

But he would hurt her. That much was certain. She might be paying lip service to the "quiet and casual" plan, but the truth was she was already falling too far, too fast. And she didn't know how to stop it. Or if she wanted to, even if it meant heartbreak at the end of the road.

He slid his hand to the small of her back. "Any other objections?"

As much as she wanted to, she couldn't think of one. Especially not with the long length of his erection pressing against her thigh.

"Nothing, eh?" He trailed kisses along her jawline. "Good."

The trail ended at her mouth, which he took ruthlessly, coaxing it open with his tongue. It touched hers, wet and warm, and she sighed into him. He tasted like mint and wicked, wicked sex, and she was instantly drunk on him.

"Straddle me," he moaned when they came up for air. "I want to feel you."

"Your leg…"

"Will be fine with you on top, running the show."

"Are you sure?" She rose onto her knees.

"Wait." He grabbed her hips.

"Did I hurt you?" She bit her lip. "See? I told you this was a bad idea."

"It's a brilliant idea if we get naked first."

"Naked?"

"Yeah, you know. In your birthday suit. Starkers. *Au naturel.*" Cade sat up and reached for the hem of his T-shirt. "I'll get the ball rolling, if it makes you more comfortable. But you might have to help with my shorts."

He pulled the shirt over his head and tossed it onto the floor. "Now you. Tit for tat."

"Pun intended?" Her mouth went dry and her palms itched with the need to explore every ridge and valley of his chest and abs, to burrow her fingers in the short, crisp hairs that dotted his pecs and formed a happy trail to his belly button and beyond. Unadulterated lust made her stomach turn somersaults, lust powerful enough to override her insecurities about showing off her extra fifteen—okay, twenty—pounds in the stark light of day.

"Hell yes." He laughed, making his pecs dance, and the somersaults in her stomach turned to cartwheels. "Now take it off."

She dragged her gaze from his chiseled chest and met his white-hot stare. "That's romantic."

"You want romance? How's this for romance?" His hands circled her waist and he pulled her on top of him. "You drive me crazy. I can't stop thinking about you. I look at you, and I don't see Ivy, my best friend's sis-

ter. Or Ivy, the girl who crank-called the principal on a
dare and asked him to confirm his order of ten strippers
for a pep rally. I see Ivy, the woman who built a successful career on her own terms. Who loves her family
so much she put that career on hold when they needed
her. Who makes the sexiest little whimpers and moans
when she comes."

Her insides dissolved into a puddle of feels. How had
he known exactly what she needed to hear? That their
past was in the past. That he wanted the woman she
was now.

"Well, since you put it that way…" She lifted her shirt
over her stomach, her breasts and finally her head. It
joined his on the floor, followed by her bra. Desire un-
dulated around them in waves, like a force field shielding them from the outside world.

"Damn." Cade's heated gaze moved from her face
to her chest.

Ivy balled her hands into fists at her sides, fighting
the urge to cover herself. "What are you waiting for?"

"I'm deciding where to start. Here?" His fingers caressed the soft undersides of her breasts. "Or maybe
here."

He brushed her nipples with his thumbs, forcing a
moan from her throat.

"Here, there, anywhere." She arched into him. "As
long as you're touching me, I don't care."

He chuckled. "You sound like Dr. Seuss."

"I don't think he wrote anything that even remotely
covers this situation."

"Probably not." Cade lowered his head and planted
a kiss on the side of her throat. The wet pressure of his

mouth worked a shudder through her from the inside out. "We'll have to write our own playbook. You up for it?"

"If you are."

He rocked against her. His erection was huge and hard and hot. "What do you think?"

She dropped her head forward, her hair falling across her face. "I think I'm going to like having a roommate."

11

CADE LOOKED AT Ivy astride him, her auburn hair back to its natural, untamed state, her hazel eyes glazed over with desire. His dick was so hard it hurt. An aching need pulsed through his veins and the air squeezed out of his lungs. Had he ever wanted anyone this badly?

He slid a finger under the waistband of her yoga pants. He'd never thought these things were sexy before, but the way they hugged Ivy's hips and ass made him think dirty thoughts about how he'd like to grab onto those hips while she rode him into next week. Still, the pants had to go. He tugged at them.

"I'll do it." She climbed off him. "You're injured."

"Not that injured."

"I'm running this show, remember?"

"Yes, ma'am." He pushed a hand through his hair and leaned back against the arm of the sofa. "You're the boss."

She slid her pants down to her ankles and kicked them aside. "Now you."

He lifted his hips and she inched his shorts down his

thighs. The little touches as she worked her way over his knees to the top of his cast left a trail of sparks.

"Now comes the tricky part." She frowned, creating adorably concerned wrinkles on her forehead. "I don't want to hurt you."

"The only way you're going to hurt me is if you stop."

"Don't say I didn't warn you."

She eased the shorts over his cast and off his feet. He should have felt exposed and vulnerable, lying naked and incapacitated, his cock jutting up like a flagpole. Instead, all he felt was anxious and needy and more turned on than an air conditioner in July.

"See? It wasn't that hard."

She eyed his erection. "I beg to differ."

The pit of his belly tightened. "Why don't you climb aboard and prove your point."

With a husky laugh, she straddled him again, taking his cock in her hand. She licked her lips as she moved her fingers up and down his shaft. "It's pretty hard, all right."

"Think you can do something about that?"

"I can try."

Gingerly, she slid down his body and bent her head to touch her tongue to his crown. She lapped up a bead of moisture, and he groaned long and loud.

"That's a damn good start." He gripped her shoulder.

She wrapped her lips around him and took him inch by tortuous inch to the back of her throat, sucking hard and fast. Fuck, she was good at this. Just the way he liked it, nice and wet with the right amount of pressure and plenty of tongue action, her hand and mouth working together in perfect rhythm. Every so often she pulled back and circled the head, stopping each time she reached the sensitive tissue on the underside of his penis and flicking it with the tip of her tongue.

He closed his eyes, shutting out the image of her glossy, bee-stung lips on his cock, and fought the urge to thrust up into that perfect mouth. If he did, the extreme pleasure, the intense personal connection between them, would be over all too soon. And no matter what the doctor said about him needing rest, he felt like he could go for hours.

Ivy released him with a *pop* and sighed. "You taste good. But I need you inside me."

He opened his eyes to find her crawling back up his body, her hair shadowing her face. "No complaint here."

She lifted herself over him.

"Wait." He groaned out the word, not wanting to stop. "Condom."

The momentarily confused look on her face was replaced with relief. "I'm on the pill. And I'm clean."

"So am I." He cupped the sweet globes of her ass and squeezed. "Thank God."

Slowly, achingly, she lowered herself onto his cock, and he slid into her hot, tight core. The desire to drive into her was too strong now, and he gave in to it, arching his hips upward. Big mistake. He turned his head, trying to cover a wince at the dull ache in his leg.

"Let me." Ivy pushed him back down and started to move over him, lifting, falling, grinding. Her head fell back and with it her hair, letting him see her expression: eyes glassy, lips parted, cheeks flush with passion.

"God, Ivy, that's... It feels..." *What? Amazing? Erotic? Sexy as fuck?* Nothing he could come up with seemed enough to describe the raw, unfamiliar sensation traveling through his body like a bolt of lightning.

"I know." She planted her hands on his chest and continued to ride him, understanding even without words. "Me, too."

"Don't stop," he panted. "I'll die if you stop."

"Not part of my plan."

She rose and he pushed into her, hard and deep, stretching her, filling her. He grabbed her hips and pumped into her, the discomfort in his leg a distant second to his need to please her, possess her. It only took a few thrusts before the first vibrations of her orgasm made her shudder and contract, squeezing him. He clenched his teeth, fighting hard not to come until her climax was spent.

When the last spasm had racked her body, he turned her until they were on their sides, making sure his bad leg was on top, propped up by the pillow. Still deep inside her, he looked into her eyes, withdrew, then plunged even deeper. "Put your leg around my waist."

"But your cast…"

"Will be fine." He rested his forehead on hers. "Put your leg around me. I need to feel you."

He plunged again and she sucked in a breath. "You are feeling me."

"Closer," he moaned into her mouth.

"Yes." She looped her leg over his waist, pulling him in.

He drove into her faster, harder, deeper. Again and again, until he felt the squeeze of her second orgasm, even tighter than before.

She cried out his name and gripped him hard as she came apart around him. His fingers dug into her hips and he continued his assault, seeking the same release.

She gazed up at him with those lust-glazed, postorgasm eyes, and he was gone. A fierce, all-consuming pleasure ripped through him, starting somewhere deep within and radiating down his erection until his own orgasm ripped through him like a flash fire.

"Is it me?" he asked when he finally caught his breath. "Or does it get better every time?"

"It's not you." She started to slide her leg off him.

"Don't move." He tightened his arms around her. "Not yet."

She relaxed in his embrace and he crushed her to his sweat-slicked chest. Whatever had just happened felt different, bigger, more important somehow than whatever it was they'd been doing before. And he wasn't ready to let it—or her—go anytime soon.

"WHICH ONE DO you want?" Sykes held up two video games. "*Call of Duty: Black Ops 3* or *Super Mario Kart*?"

"*Super Mario.*" Hansen came in from the kitchen juggling four bottles of Heineken.

"I wasn't asking you." Sykes set down the games on the coffee table, snagged one of the bottles from Hansen and popped off the top. "The gimp gets to choose."

"I thought it was the hero gets to choose," Cade countered.

"Have it your way, if it makes you feel better," Sykes joked. "So what'll it be?"

"*Black Ops.*" Cade took the bottle Hansen handed him, opened it and chugged about half of it. "I need to shoot something."

He put down the bottle on the coffee table with a *thunk* in between the video games and his propped-up leg. Two weeks as an invalid had him on edge. Couch-potato living was so not for him.

Trey poked his head out from behind the television. "You sure Ivy won't mind me hooking up your Xbox? I mean, it's not like you're really living together, right?"

"Maybe that's why he needs to shoot something." Hansen sat next to Cade, took a sip from his own beer and put the remaining bottle down on the coffee table. "Sexual frustration."

"I thought you two were dating."

"Did you do something to piss her off?"

"Is she holding out on you?"

"Got a case of the blue balls, buddy?"

"You guys are idiots." Cade swigged his beer.

"Idiots who aren't going to stop asking until you tell us what's going on with you and Ivy." Sykes leaned against the wall next to the television, watching Trey, who'd gone back to work on the Xbox.

"Yeah," Hansen agreed. "We gotta know what to tell Sasha when she comes sniffing around the station again."

Cade tensed. "Sasha's been to the station?"

Damn. He thought she'd finally given up on him after the whole display at the ball game.

"Once or twice," Sykes hedged.

"More like five times." Hansen was all too eager to correct his partner. "She's driving Cappy nuts."

"Don't worry." Sykes gave Cade a reassuring smile from across the room. "You're secret's safe with us. We didn't tell her where you're staying."

"Even when she tried to bribe us with baked goods." Hansen closed his eyes and inhaled, as if whatever the hell she'd made was right there in front of him, then released his breath on a long, slow sigh. "For a woman the size of a stick figure, she sure can cook."

"But you know how this town is," Trey chimed in from his hiding place, still trying to sort out the tangle of wires coming from the game console. "She's bound to find out eventually."

"I haven't been broadcasting my whereabouts, but it's not exactly a secret." Cade frowned. "Everyone at the hospital knows. You guys. Ivy's family."

She'd managed to convince them that this living arrangement was purely platonic. Whether he could do the same with his buddies remained to be seen.

"True, but the last thing you need is your psycho ex finding you here with Ivy," Hansen said. "Especially if you two have been playing house."

"Getting cozy." Sykes waggled his brows.

"Bumping uglies." Hansen nudged Cade with his elbow.

Sykes narrowed his eyes. "Which you oh-so-skillfully avoided confirming."

"All set." Trey crawled out from behind the TV. "We should be good to go."

Hansen shook his head. "Not until lover boy here tells us whether he and Ivy are doing the horizontal mambo."

"Oh, for Christ's sake, grow up." Cade finished off his beer and slammed it down on the coffee table with more force than necessary. It was a miracle the bottle didn't break. "Ivy's a friend. She's taking care of me."

And helping him study for the lieutenant exam, like she'd promised. Not that he was admitting that to these goofballs.

"In more ways than one, I'll bet." Sykes flopped

into an easy chair and absently peeled the label off his Heineken.

"Friends with benefits," Hansen agreed.

"Leave him alone." Trey muscled Hansen off the couch, handed Cade one of the game controllers and sat next to him with the other. "Besides, I happen to know for a fact that the answer to your question is yes."

"How the hell do you know that?" Cade pinned him with a piercing stare. He hadn't told *anyone* what he was doing with Ivy. Hell, he wasn't even sure himself.

Trey shrugged and reached for his beer. "We've been friends since college. I can tell when you're getting some and when you're not. And you are definitely getting some."

"Is it my postcoital glow?" Cade batted his eyelashes, his tone dripping with sarcasm.

"We're not girls, asshole." Trey lifted the bottle to his lips. "But I like you better when you're getting laid. You're a lot more fun."

So much for purely platonic.

Hansen sat cross-legged on the floor. "Now that that's settled, how about we break out the assault rifles and take out some bad guys?"

"Turn on the TV." Cade gestured to the remote on the end table next to Sykes, happy to be off the hook even if it meant his relationship with Ivy was semipublic knowledge now. "I'm feeling lucky."

They'd been playing for less than an hour—Trey had died an early death and Cade was facing off against Sykes, who'd beaten Hansen in rock-paper-scissors for the chance to take on the winner—when the front door opened and Ivy came in. Her face was red from heat and exertion, her once neat ponytail a half-collapsed mess, with strands of escaped hair sticking to her cheeks. She had a smudge of dirt on one arm and her shorts were streaked with what looked like grass stains, as were the formerly white socks sticking out of her work boots.

Yet somehow she'd never looked better, and the realization hit Cade in the solar plexus like a stream of water from a deluge gun.

This was more than a physical thing. He'd want this woman if she was wearing a burlap sack and covered in cow manure.

"Hey, guys." She put her purse down on a chair in the corner and greeted everyone with a wave. "I see the gang's all here."

"Uh, yeah." Cade set down his controller just as his on-screen alter ego got annihilated by a gunship. "I hope that's not a problem."

"Not at all. I'm glad to see you have company. It must get boring for you here alone all day when I'm working." She undid her ponytail and shook her hair out, reminding him of how it looked splayed across the pillow as he brought her to the peak again, her body writhing and thrashing beneath him.

Suddenly the damn company couldn't leave soon enough.

Trey caught Cade's eye and stood. "We should get going."

"Stay for dinner." Ivy motioned for him to sit back down. "I'll order pizza."

"Valentino's?" Hansen asked.

"Meat lovers?" suggested Sykes.

Clueless idiots.

"Is there any other?" Ivy gathered her hair back up

and twisted the band around it. A few strands still managed to escape.

"Their bacon-and-onion's not bad, either," Trey said, slowly lowering himself back onto the couch with a look to Cade that said, "Sorry, man. Pizza before pussy."

Traitor.

"I'll get one of each." She picked up a grocery bag Cade hadn't even noticed her carry in. "And I brought some more beer. Heineken, right? And a six-pack of Guinness in case anyone wanted a stout. I'll go put it in the fridge and order the pies. That'll give me time for a quick shower before they come."

She disappeared into the kitchen.

"Damn." Trey's eyes followed her departure a little too closely for Cade's liking. "Pizza and beer. There goes the perfect woman."

As much as he wanted to lock his friend in a closet and throw away the key, Cade couldn't argue with him one bit.

12

"ANYBODY HOME?"

Ivy stood just inside the front door, the house eerily quiet. Uneasy goose bumps prickled her skin, making the hair on her arms stand on end.

For the past few weeks, she'd come home to the TV blaring, or music playing, or male laughter—or cursing—mixed with gunfire from the Xbox. It was scary how quickly she'd gotten used to the noise. So much so that its absence made her uncomfortable.

"Cade?" She headed into the living room. Maybe he was taking a nap. Or maybe the guys had come by and gotten him out of the house for a change. He was in a walking cast now, and the doctor said he could resume light activity, although he didn't think Cade was ready to tackle the two flights of steep, narrow stairs to his apartment yet. They'd probably taken him to the Half Pint for some watered-down beer and a game of darts or pool.

Or maybe he'd fallen and hit his head and had been lying unconscious on her bathroom floor for hours. It was supposed to be the most dangerous room in the house...

"Cade?" She quickened her steps to the point where she was almost running. "Are you okay?"

"In here." His voice came from the dining room just off the kitchen. "But don't come in yet. I'm not ready."

"Ready for what?" What was he doing in there? They never used the dining room. Most nights they ate dinner at the big oak table in the kitchen or in front of the TV.

Just like an old married couple. She shook off the ridiculous thought.

"It's a surprise," he answered. She heard what sounded like glass breaking, and he swore. "I'm all right. And don't worry. I'll replace your sister's casserole dish."

"No big deal." Ivy tossed her pocketbook onto the easy chair. "I'm sure she won't even miss it."

"Sit down. Relax. There's a glass of pinot grigio and a plate of bruschetta on the coffee table. I'll come get you in a few minutes."

For the first time since she entered the house, she noticed that the lights were turned down low. Two scented candles burned in decorative jars on the table next to a wineglass and platter of toasted bread topped with mozzarella and tomato. She flopped onto the couch, kicked off her Chuck Taylors and took a deep breath.

Orange and cinnamon. Nice. Soothing.

She tipped back her head and closed her eyes. It had been a busy day at the nursery, followed by another birthday party, this one for a rambunctious three-year-old. As good as the bruschetta looked, a catnap was screaming her name. Just a few minutes of shut-eye—and maybe a quick shower, she thought, scratching at a bug bite on her elbow. Then she'd have her second wind and be ready for whatever Cade had in store for her.

She was halfway to dreamland when his voice broke through her semislumber. "Hey there, Rip Van Winkle."

She groaned and covered her eyes with her forearm. "So that's how you see me. A hundred and fifty years old with a beard down to my waist."

"Right." His voice was a low, sultry drawl and she let it wash over her. "That's exactly how I saw you last night when I was deep in your sweet pussy."

A flush crept up her cheeks. One of the things she'd learned about Cade was that he liked to talk dirty. And one of the things she'd learned about herself was that she liked when he did.

Ivy lowered her arm to find him looming over her, his blue eyes smoldering. He looked ridiculously appealing and extremely sexy at the same time in khaki cargo shorts, a powder-blue T-shirt and a bright yellow apron with a picture of a penguin in a chef's hat that read I Kiss Better Than I Cook.

"Not exactly a ringing endorsement of your culinary skills."

"I don't know." He looked down at the apron then back at her. "I'm a damn good kisser."

"Says who?"

"Says your screams and moans."

Her face burned hotter. "I do not scream."

"So you admit you moan."

"I admit nothing." She blinked herself awake and sat up. "Are you going to tell me what this is all about or what?"

"I've got a better idea." He held out a hand to her. "How about I show you instead?"

She took his hand and stood, catching sight of her freak-show hair and sweaty face, complete with a dab of birthday cake on her nose, in the mirror above the old player piano against the far wall. "Can I take a shower first?"

"Why don't we shower together after dinner?"

At the mention of food, her stomach let out an embarrassing grumble, reminding her that she'd passed up lunch in her rush to get to the birthday party. She plucked a piece of bruschetta off the plate and popped it into her mouth. The flavors of the fresh tomato and mozzarella, mixed with hints of garlic, basil and even a touch of crushed red pepper, exploded on her taste buds. "Holy crap, that's good. Where did you learn to cook like that?"

He shrugged. "We all take turns at the station. Plus, like your mom always says…"

She joined him in repeating one of her mother's favorite sayings. "If you can read, you can cook."

She snared her wineglass and took a sip. The crisp, refreshing pinot grigio was the perfect complement to the rich, ripe taste of the bruschetta. "If the main course is half as good as the appetizer, I can hold off on the shower. Even if it means I have to wait to see you naked."

He held a hand to his heart and staggered back as if he'd been shot. "You wound me. Choosing food over fornication."

"A girl's gotta do what a girl's gotta do." She took another look in the mirror and cringed. "But I should at least wash my hands and face and run a brush through my hair."

"You look perfect to me. But go ahead, if you insist. Just don't take too long. Dinner's almost ready."

As if on cue, the oven timer went off. Cade blew out the candles and shuffled into the kitchen. Ivy broke the land speed record washing up and whipping her hair into shape before joining him in the dining room.

"Wow. This looks…amazing."

He'd gone through a lot of effort, that much was certain. Instead of candles, he'd used strands of white lights for romantic effect, stringing them overhead from one side of the room to the other and dangling them in the windows behind the sheer curtains. The table was covered with a lace tablecloth he'd found who knows where, and in the center stood a vase of gerbera daisies that looked like they'd been freshly cut from the garden out back, lit from beneath with soft, blue LEDs. Somehow, he'd even managed to scrounge up two settings of her grandmother's old Wedgewood and topped them with cloth napkins, folded into fans. Wooden holders held Scrabble tiles from the ancient set in the cabinet under the stairs, spelling out their names next to each plate.

"I'm glad you like it." He pulled out the chair in front of the plate with her name beside it and gestured for her to sit.

"How did you do all this?" she asked, following his lead and taking a seat.

"I had a little help from my friends. Hansen hung the lights, Sykes put together the centerpiece and Trey was my sous chef. He left just before you got here. But the napkins were all me. I watched this chick do it on YouTube." Cade beamed like a kid who'd gotten a gold star on his report card. "Martha something-or-another."

Ivy chuckled. "Martha Stewart?"

"Yeah. That's her."

"Why?"

"Why did I watch that Martha chick? Because she's good at this stuff. She can make a freaking swan." He shook his head in a mix of disbelief and admiration. "A swan. I tried. It's hard. It took me an hour to get the fans right."

"Not her. This." Ivy waved an arm around the room, gesturing at the lights, the centerpiece, the Scrabble place markers.

"I wanted to say thank you." He reached across the table to lift a bottle from a marble wine chiller and topped off her glass.

She took a sip. "For taking you in?"

"That." He put the bottle back in the chiller. "And for putting up with all my bad habits."

"Bad habits?"

"Leaving the toilet seat up. Forgetting to put the cap on the toothpaste. Having friends over without asking first."

"Oh, that." She raised her glass in a mock toast. "It's nothing."

"It's not nothing. You were great with the guys. They really like you." He trailed a finger down her arm, bare below her shirtsleeve, and she shivered, almost spilling her wine.

"I like them, too." She set down the glass before she dropped it altogether. "Well, maybe not Trey so much. Did you know he has a poster of the Kardashian sisters in his bedroom? All three of them."

Cade arched a brow at her. "The more important question is how do you know?"

"He told me. Said I reminded him of a redheaded Kourtney. Or maybe it was Kim. I always mix them up."

"His idea of a compliment, I'm sure."

Her uncooperative stomach chose that moment to rumble again.

"Is that your way of letting me know you're ready for the first course?" Cade teased.

"First course?" She gaped at him. "How many are there?"

"Four." He ticked them off on his fingers. "There's the bruschetta, salad, main course and wait until you see what's for dessert."

"Well, then." She unfolded her napkin—as much as she hated destroying his Martha Stewart–worthy handiwork—and set it in her lap. "I guess we'd better get started."

"How's that?" Cade tightened the blindfold around Ivy's head. "Can you see anything?"

"No." She put a shaky hand up to the black silk covering her eyes. "Not a thing."

"Good." He took both her hands in his and pulled her to her feet. "Nervous?"

"I don't know." She licked her lips. "Should I be? I've never had someone blindfold me to eat dessert before."

"Trust me. You're going to like this." He stepped backward, leading her.

"Where are we going?"

"Not far."

"You're not planning anything kinky, are you?"

"I plead the Fifth." He stopped in front of the sofa and eased her down onto it. "Now sit still and be quiet. You ask too many questions."

"Will it involve whipped cream and genitalia?"

"What did I just say about asking questions?" He smiled, then, remembering she couldn't see him, leaned down and brushed a kiss across her lips. "Don't move.

I'll be right back. And no peeking. That would mean you don't trust me, and we can't have that, can we?"

"We certainly can't," she agreed, her voice laced with sarcasm.

He whistled as he retreated to the kitchen. A few minutes later he returned with a tray of assorted desserts. He'd sent Hansen, the only one of the bunch he could trust to be discreet, to the Rolling Pin with instructions to bring back "something sexy." His friend had procured a box labeled "petits fours"—tiny cakes and éclairs, little tarts and pastries. Then Cade had added a couple of touches of his own.

He set the tray on the coffee table and sat next to Ivy. "This may get a little messy. You should take that pretty top off."

"This old thing?" She flicked the hem. "It was at the bottom of my drawer. I only wore it because I haven't done laundry this week."

"Still, I'd hate to ruin it."

"If you insist."

"I do."

She lifted the shirt over her head and dropped it onto the couch behind her, leaving her in a lacy, pale pink bra that barely contained her double Ds. It was so sheer he could see right through to her nipples, which practically poked holes through the fabric, telling him she was as turned on by their game as he was.

And it was just beginning.

"Better?" she asked, breathless.

"Much." He reached around her to make sure the blindfold was still secure. "But not good enough. Lose the bra."

"I won't argue with you there." She undid the clasp

and let the straps slide down her arms. "I spent a fortune on this thing."

"And I'll bet you have matching panties, too."

The bra fell away and she was naked from the waist up. "Mmm-hmm. A scrap of silk, held up by two flimsy ribbons. Wanna see?"

He did. He loved her frilly, impractical undergarments. A total contrast to the mostly conservative clothes she covered them with. Like the woman herself. All business on the outside but naughty underneath.

But they had plenty of time for that. Tonight was all about Ivy, about pampering her, about making her feel wanton and reckless and desirable.

"One step at a time, sweetheart." He picked up a cream puff, scooped up a dab of the filling with his finger and ran it over her lips. "Hungry?"

"Depends what for."

"For this."

He coated his finger with filling and brought it to her mouth. She took it inside and sucked and swiped until it was clean, sending a jolt of lust directly to his crotch and making his dick stand at attention.

"Good?" he growled.

"Delicious. You should try some."

She sighed and leaned her head back against the couch, and he was almost positive that under the blindfold her eyes were wide and glassy with desire. Not that it was coming off anytime soon. He was having way too much fun, and so was she.

"I think I will."

He smeared the rest of the filling around first one areola then the other, finishing them off with a dollop atop each nipple. "You don't mind if I use you as a table, do you, darling?"

"A little late to ask now, isn't it?"

"Oops." He swiped at the underside of one breast with his tongue, catching a bit of the cream. Sweet, but not as sweet as her creamy flesh. "My bad."

"All is forgiven if you keep doing that."

"This?" He cupped her breasts in his palms and took another swipe. "That's just a warm-up. This is the main attraction."

His mouth closed over one nipple.

"Please." She grasped at his shoulders. "You're driving me crazy."

"Like I said, I'm just getting started, babe. Maybe you could distract yourself. Think about shutter speeds or aspect ratios or something."

"How do you know what an aspect ratio is?"

"See?" He chucked against her soft skin. "It's working already."

He moved to the other breast. She moaned then gasped as he nipped her with his teeth. He continued to torture her, drawing her into his mouth and lapping and suckling until she was making soft, mewing sounds. She returned the favor, making him groan by slipping her hands under his shirt and threading them through the hair on his chest.

"Can I take the blindfold off now?" She arched into him, her roaming hands stopping to play with his nipples.

"Not just yet." He reached for a jar of honey, still warm from the microwave. "I've got another surprise for you."

"You're not the only one."

An angry, male voice made the hairs on the back of Cade's neck prickle. He instinctively moved to shield Ivy, who squealed.

With one hand, she grabbed for her shirt to cover herself while ripping off the blindfold. "Jesus Christ, Gabe. Haven't you ever heard of knocking?"

"What the hell is going on here?" Gabe barked, ignoring his sister. Cade started to respond, but his soon-to-be-former best friend cut him off with a slashing gesture that probably mimed what he'd like to do to Cade's private parts. "Don't answer that. I can see for myself."

"I repeat—" Ivy pulled her shirt on with short, jerky movements "—do you not know how to knock?"

"I *did* knock. You two were so lost in the throes of passion you didn't hear me."

Gabe went into his take-no-prisoners prosecutor mode, his steely eyes focused on Cade and his hands clenched into fists. Cade braced himself for the interrogation.

"How long have you been screwing her? Since you've been living here? Before?"

"Hey." Cade put a protective arm around Ivy. "That's your sister you're talking about."

"I know." If possible, Gabe's eyes grew even colder. His mouth stretched into a hard, thin line across his face. "Do you?"

He turned his attention to Ivy. "Do you know this guy goes through women like tissues? Is that what you want? To be another notch in his tissue box?"

"That's enough." Cade stood and faced off with his friend. "I'm not doing this here. Not in front of Ivy."

"Fine." Gabe stuffed his clenched fists into his pockets. "You. Me. The Half Pint. Thirty minutes."

He turned on his heel, the slam of the door echoing behind him as he stormed out of the house.

13

IT WAS MORE like forty minutes later by the time Cade had helped Ivy clean up things and convinced her that her brother wouldn't kill him—even though he wasn't too sure about that himself. Gabe sat alone at one end of the bar, an almost empty glass in front of him, his scowl keeping the other patrons at bay.

Cade hauled himself up onto a stool and waved the bartender over. "Ghost Island Double IPA for me. And another of whatever my friend's having."

"Friends don't fuck family." Gabe sucked down the rest of his drink and slammed the empty glass on the bar top.

The bartender snatched it up and sidled away, shooting Cade a look that said, "Not cool, dude. Not. Cool."

Great. Two against one.

"Stop saying that," Cade hissed through gritted teeth when the bartender was out of earshot. "That's not what I'm doing with your sister."

"You expect me to believe you haven't had sex with her?" Gabe's voice dripped with disdain. "What I saw seemed pretty intimate to me."

"I didn't say that. But we're not just having sex."

"What's that supposed to mean?"

Damned if he knew.

The bartender returned with their drinks before Cade could form an answer. He took a long pull of the IPA, praying for some Dutch courage. Or divine inspiration.

"What it means," he said finally, "is that Ivy's different from the other women I've dated."

"My point exactly, asshole." Gabe swirled the amber liquid in his glass then sipped. "You can't love her then leave her like you do with all the rest."

"I'm not the one doing the leaving."

"What do you mean?"

"Your sister's bags are packed the minute your father doesn't need her anymore."

"And you want her to stay in Stockton?"

Leave it to Gabe to get right to the heart of the matter. Did he want her to stay? Would she even consider it if he asked? And if she said yes, would she eventually come to resent him for making her give up her big-time career? The two people who were supposed to be the most important in his life had chosen their work over him. What if Ivy proved to be no better than his parents?

"Let me ask you something." Cade shredded a bar napkin, stalling, fully aware he was venturing into dangerous territory. "When did you know with Devin?"

"Know what?"

"That she was the one."

Gabe set down his glass ever so slowly. His words, when he spoke, were just as deliberate. "You think my sister might be the one?"

"Just answer the damn question."

"It's hard to say." Gabe's eyes clouded over and his

mouth curled into a wistful smile. "But I think my heart knew that night I found Devin in Central Park, kicking the crap out of Fast Fingers Freddie. My head just took a little longer to get with the program."

"Fast Fingers Freddie?" Cade almost choked on his IPA.

"I never told you that story?"

"I'd remember if you had."

"Some other time." Gabe took another sip from his glass. "I'm not here to discuss my love life. I'm here to find out what the hell the guy I thought was my best friend is doing messing around with my sister."

"I told you. I'm not messing around with her." Cade balled up the napkin bits and deposited them on the bar. "I like her."

"I've seen what happens to the women you like." Gabe eyeballed Cade over the rim of his glass. "A month, two tops, and you kick them to the curb."

"In two months, Ivy will be long gone. Back to her high-fashion-photographer lifestyle. And I'll be here, doing what I do best. Fighting fires. Rescuing cats."

"Which leads me back to my earlier question. Do you want her to stay?"

Cade had ducked it once, but Gabe wasn't letting him off the hook. "I wish it was that easy."

"It can be." Gabe drained his drink. The bartender grabbed a bottle of Johnnie Walker Black and moved in for a refill, but Gabe covered the glass with his hand and shook his head. "If you're really serious about my sister and not just jerking her around."

Cade slapped a palm on the bar. "How many times do I have to tell you, dammit? I'm not jerking Ivy around. I like having her in my life. She gets me. The real me.

Not Cade Hardesty, good-time guy. Did I tell you she's helping me study for the lieutenant exam? She thinks I've got a decent chance of passing, too. She's the first woman who's ever seen me as more than a pretty face and an easy lay."

He paused to let the words sink in, to absorb their real meaning. This was more than friendship, more than sex. How much more, he wasn't sure, but after a minute, his mouth was ready to voice what his heart was just beginning to realize. "I think I might be falling in love with her."

"Shit." Gabe leaned back on his stool and studied Cade. "You are serious."

"As a heart attack." Cade reached down to scratch under his cast. "Or a broken leg."

"You know she's had a thing for you like forever."

"What?"

"Seriously, man. Were you blind, deaf and dumb in high school? She followed you around like a puppy dog."

Cade grimaced and finished off his IPA. "I was dumb, that's for sure."

"What do you mean 'was'?"

"Very funny."

Gabe rested his elbows on the bar. "She'll stay, if you ask her."

"What if she says no?"

"What if she doesn't?"

"Okay, then." Cade rubbed the back of his neck. "What if she says yes and two or three or ten years down the line she realizes what a colossal idiot she was abandoning a glamorous career for a small-town firefighter?"

"What if she says yes and you live happily ever after?" Gabe clapped a hand on Cade's shoulder. "Look,

I can't tell you what's going to happen. But I can tell you this—my sister's worth the risk. If you love her, or even think you might love her, and don't do something about it, you'll regret it."

Cade understood risk. He risked his life every time he ran into a building burning. But risking his life was one thing. Risking his heart was another.

"So what's it gonna be, pal?" Gabe asked. "Are you gonna man up and tell her how you feel, like you told me to do just a few months ago in this very bar? Or are you going to be a wimp and let her walk away?"

"Thanks for throwing my own words back in my face."

"Anytime." The hand on Cade's shoulder tightened. "Now answer the question. Are you a man or a mouse?"

"I'm working on it." Cade pulled out his wallet and threw down two tens on the bar. "But when I figure it out, I promise you'll be the second to know."

"Good." Gabe added a bill to the pile. "Just promise me one more thing."

"What's that?"

"Don't hurt her. Because if you do, I'd have to hurt you. And I'd hate to mess up that pretty face."

THE CLOCK ON the nightstand in the guest room, where she'd slept since Cade moved in, read 9:30 a.m. Well past her normal rising hour, but Ivy wasn't going anywhere anytime soon. Not without any parties, proms or pets to photograph, the part-timer she'd hired covering the morning shift at the nursery and Cade wrapped around her like a second skin, one arm flung across her midriff, his legs entwined with hers.

It had been well past midnight when she felt the mattress dip and the heat of Cade's body surround her. He'd muttered something that sounded suspiciously like "not a wimp" and proceeded to fall almost immediately asleep, no doubt thanks to the alcohol on his breath.

Typical. Boys bonding over brews. Better than her brother beating the crap out of her boyfriend.

If that's what Cade was.

Neither one of them had felt the need to define their relationship, but would that change now that Gabe was in on their secret? It was only a matter of time before her parents found out. What was she going to tell them? That she and Cade were fuck buddies?

Ivy frowned as she pictured her stern Scandinavian father's reaction to that news. If Cade thought Gabe had been angry...

She closed her eyes and inhaled the mix of soap and sweat and citrus, which had become as familiar to her as breathing, that was uniquely Cade. She wasn't going to worry about the future, not when she had him warm and willing in her bed. Sometimes dreams did come true. And on those rare occasions when they did, she'd learned not to second-guess them.

Eyes still closed, she explored his sleeping form with her hands. Strong, broad shoulders. Thickly muscled back. She paused for a millisecond at the waistband of his boxers, then slipped her hands underneath to squeeze his beautifully biteable butt.

"Don't stop there, sweetheart," Cade growled into the nape of her neck. "The behind may be fine, but there's a party going on in front."

As if to prove his point, he tilted his hips so she could feel his hardening erection against her.

"So I see." She moved her hands lower, cupping the

globes of his ass and pulling him closer to her. "What do you propose we do about it?"

"That depends on how much time we have."

"I don't know. Is my brother going to barge in here again, or did you two reach some sort of détente last night?"

"Let's just say we came to an understanding. He won't be bothering us anymore."

"Then it looks like we've got all day."

"All day?" He lifted his head to look at her. "No mounds of mulch to move? No fiestas to photograph?"

"Not a one." She stared back at him, a smile inching across her face. Hell's bells, he was gorgeous, with his cornflower-blue eyes, plump, kissable lips and strong, masculine jaw, dotted with morning stubble. All hers, for the time being.

"Good." He kissed her, quick and dirty with just a hint of tongue to stoke the fire building inside her. "Consider yourself chained to this bed."

"Literally or figuratively?"

"Whichever you prefer." He peppered her neck with little love bites.

"How will I eat?"

"I'll feed you."

He nibbled his way down to the top of her cleavage. "I intend to keep you fully occupied between the sheets."

She caught her breath as his tongue stole deeper into the crevice between her breasts. Heat spread through her body like molten lava. "Has anyone ever told you you're a sex fiend?"

"Yes." He nudged aside the collar of her tank top so he could explore further. "But I'm not the one with my hands down someone's pants."

"Good point. They have to go."

"Your hands?"

"Your pants."

"I could get on board with that plan." He raised his hips so she could slide off his boxers. Gloriously naked and fully erect, he threw off the covers and stretched out next to her, eyeing the tank top and panties she'd slept in. "You're overdressed."

"Easily fixed." She reached for the hem of her top but froze when she heard the familiar strains of the Veronicas' "Mother Mother" from her cell phone.

"Let it ring," Cade moaned, putting his hands over hers and starting to pull off the top himself.

"Can't." She rolled out of his grasp and groped for the phone, which she'd left on the nightstand. "That's my mom's ringtone. She wouldn't call unless it was an emergency. She's the one who suggested I take the day off."

That was putting it mildly. More like browbeat her into submission, even going so far as to coerce the part-timer into filling in.

"Your dad?" Cade asked, voicing her fears.

"Maybe." Ivy found the phone and swiped the screen. "The doctors say he's getting better every day, but…"

But what did they really know. What did anyone know? Life was unpredictable. Unexpected. Too short to be wasted. Wasn't that why she was taking this gamble with Cade?

"Mom?" Ivy put the phone to her ear. "Is Dad—"

"He's fine, *topolina*," her mother interrupted. "But I have a problem."

Outwardly, Ivy breathed a sigh of relief that her father was okay. Inside, she cringed at her mother's nickname for her. She'd never been sweet or little, nor had she ever been remotely like a mouse. But some long-gone Italian great-aunt had pinned it on her at birth and it had stuck for her mother.

"Can it wait until tomorrow?" Ivy asked, sneaking a glance at Cade, sprawled on the bed like a big, beautiful tomcat, waiting to have his belly rubbed.

Or something else rubbed.

"Unfortunately, no." Her mother's unusually clipped voice brought Ivy back to the conversation at hand. "Today is the PTA annual summer carnival. It's our biggest fund-raiser of the year."

"Yes, I know." Ivy bit back a smile. Her mother had retired from teaching at the local elementary school a few years ago to work with her husband at the nursery full-time, but that didn't mean she didn't still have a hand in every bake sale, raffle and pancake breakfast. "What does that have to do with me?"

"Nothing until about five minutes ago. We need someone to man the photo booth. That *cretino* Florian Rhodes called and canceled. Said he was double-booked."

"I told you not to hire him."

"I didn't want to add to your workload. You can scold me later. Can you help me now?"

Ivy took one last, longing look at Cade. "Just tell me where and when."

"The town green in half an hour."

"Half an hour?" Ivy leaped up from the bed.

"As soon as you can get there will be fine."

"Gee, thanks." Ivy paced the room.

"I'm sorry, *topolina*." Her mother had the decency to at least sound contrite. "I'm sure you were looking forward to your day off with Cade."

"With Cade?" Ivy's stomach plummeted and she froze midstride. Not even twenty-four hours. She was going to kill Gabe. How much had her big-mouthed twin told their parents?

"Well, he's staying with you while he's recovering, isn't he? Maybe you two can come over for dinner tonight. I'll make manicotti. It's Cade's favorite."

"Uh, sure, Ma." Ivy's heart slowed from runaway freight train to leaping gazelle. There was no way her old-world mother, with her traditional family values, would be catering to Cade if she knew he was screwing her daughter six ways to Sunday. "I'd better say goodbye if I'm going to make it on time. See you soon."

She ended the call and turned to see Cade propped up on his elbows, still naked as the day he was born. Naked and magnificent, all smooth, golden skin and lean muscle.

Damn, this was going to be difficult.

He rolled to his back, crossing his corded arms behind his head. "I guess I'm not chaining you to the bed, literally or figuratively."

"Blame Florian Rhodes."

"Who's he?" Cade asked.

She couldn't look at him. She just couldn't. Not if she had any hope of getting out the door anytime soon. She shifted her gaze to a painting above the bed. A beach scene. Water. Sand. Sky. Much better.

Not.

"He's the photographer who stood up the PTA."

"And you're stepping in?"

"It's the summer carnival. Their biggest fund-raiser of the year," she said, parroting her mother. "I couldn't say no."

"Of course you couldn't." He sat up and grabbed a shirt off the back of the chair next to the bed.

"What are you doing?"

"Getting dressed." He pulled the shirt on over his head.

"Why?"

"I'm coming with you."

She shook her head. "You don't have to do that."

"I want to."

"I'm running the photo booth all day. You'll be bored."

"I doubt it." He grabbed the pair of shorts hanging over the arm of the chair. "But if I am, so what? I'll be bored here. Alone. I might as well be bored at the carnival with you."

"Okay, but I'm putting you to work." She watched him slide on the shorts and reach for his walking brace. "Light duty."

"Fine by me, boss." He fastened the brace, stood and hobbled over to her. The liquid heat she'd felt earlier started to bubble inside her again when he took her in his arms and rested his forehead on hers. "As long as you don't have anything against fraternization between coworkers."

14

"Step right up, boys and girls, ladies and gentlemen of all ages." Cade sat on a stool at the entrance of the red-and-white striped tent that served as the photo booth, wearing a straw bowler he'd plucked from the trunk of costumes in the corner and twirling a prop cane like he was a carnival barker. "Have your picture taken with a real live hero."

Ivy snickered as she fixed her camera to the tripod. "A hero? Isn't that stretching it a bit?"

"How quickly they forget." He cast a sympathetic glance at his leg. "I was injured in the line of duty."

"Rescuing a cat."

He puffed out his chest. "Par for the course for us brave firefighters."

"You're a walking cliché." She focused the camera on the brightly painted backdrop and clicked off a couple of quick test shots.

"Ten bucks says this walking cliché gets you over a thousand dollars in the cash box by lunchtime. Two if I call Sykes to bring my turnout gear. Chicks dig the suspenders."

"Another dare?" Her hazel eyes flashed an unspoken challenge.

"Not a dare. A bet."

"You're on, hot stuff." She waved in their first customers, a pair of giggling girls who bypassed Cade for the costume trunk and its assortment of feathered hats and boas. "Call your friend and tell him to get your stuff over here pronto. The school needs every cent we can scrape up."

Three hours later, with a line that stretched down the block and almost twice what he'd predicted in the cash box, Cade declared himself the winner. Sweltering in his turnouts and worn out from posing with what seemed like every woman in Stockton between the ages of eighteen and eighty, including Maude from the diner, who'd pinched his ass, and the librarian, Mrs. Frazier, who'd tried to stick her tongue in his ear. But the winner nonetheless.

"I bow down to you." Ivy gave him a low, overexaggerated curtsy and escorted a besotted teenage couple into the booth. Unlike him, she seemed fresh as a daisy, laughing and chatting with the lovebirds as she positioned them.

He gave a weary smile to the next person in line, another octogenarian who eyed him hungrily.

What had gotten into these old broads? Were the Knights of Columbus spiking the lemonade at the concession stand?

He muttered a hasty "excuse me" to the latest bawdy biddy and ducked into the tent for a breather. How did Ivy do it? He'd always thought taking pictures was easy. Just point, click and shoot. Anyone with a cell phone could do it nowadays, right?

Wrong.

If there was anything he'd learned watching Ivy all morning, it was that photography was as much about people as it was about pixels. And Ivy was a people person. Cajoling toothless toddlers into smiling, convincing middle-aged matrons they looked like movie stars, conning reluctant husbands to wear ridiculous getups.

He was in the presence of a master. A master whose talent was wasted in Stockton.

Maybe Gabe was right. Maybe she would stay if Cade asked her to. But did that give him the right to ask?

Cade's stomach grumbled, reminding him he'd skipped breakfast. He had at least a couple more weeks with Ivy. Time to plan his next move.

"Hungry?" he asked her when she'd gotten rid of Romeo and Juliet.

"Famished." She peeked around the tent flap and eyed the line, still half a block long. "But it doesn't look like I'll be able to take a break anytime soon."

"I'll go get us something. What do you feel like? Funnel cake? Corn dog? Cotton candy?" Just the mention of food made his stomach grumble again. "All of the above?"

Her eyes flicked to his bum leg. "You don't have to do that."

"I'm not an invalid." He reached down and tapped the brace under his turnout pants. "They call it a walking cast for a reason. And you're not the only one about to pass out from starvation."

"Well, in that case…" She raised herself up on tiptoe to whisper in his ear. "Surprise me."

Her warm breath on his neck made him instantly hard. He could think of a million ways he'd like to surprise her, not one of them appropriate for a school carnival. He subtly adjusted himself through his bulky gear. "As you wish."

She smiled at the reference from *The Princess Bride* and he dropped a quick kiss on her forehead. That would have to satisfy him until he could get her alone. He didn't dare risk anything more or he might wind up bending her over and taking her right there in the tent.

With a frustrated groan, he shrugged off the suspenders of his turnout pants and reached for his T-shirt, which he'd shed at the request of a group of coeds for an extra twenty bucks.

"Not so fast, sonny."

He froze with his hand halfway to his shirt. The elderly woman at the front of the line must have gotten tired of waiting because now she was standing in the entrance to the tent, blocking his exit. "You're not getting away that easy. I've been standing out there for almost an hour. No easy feat when you're as old as I am."

She took another step into the tent, looked him up and down through her granny glasses and smacked her lips. *Uh-oh.* "But it'll be worth it to get up close and personal with a handsome young buck like yourself. Maude says you let her pinch your ass."

"So that's how you won the bet," Ivy said, coming up behind him. He could hear the smile in her voice. "Sacrificing yourself for the cause."

"That reminds me. You owe me ten dollars."

"I'll pay up." Her eyes lingered on his bare chest. "Later."

"I'm counting on it."

"Are we doing this or what?" A surprisingly strong,

gnarled hand rapped him on the arm. "I want me some of what Maude got."

Help me, he mouthed to Ivy.

Not a chance, Ivy mouthed back.

Cade grinned at the woman through gritted teeth. The food would have to wait. Again. "Tell you what, Mrs…"

"It's Miss." She batted her eyelashes at him. "Bartholomew. Letty Bartholomew."

"Okay, Miss Bartholomew. How about we skip the ass pinching and I give you a kiss on the cheek instead?"

Her already wrinkled forehead creased even more in thought. "Did Maude get a kiss?"

"No, ma'am."

"Good." She stuffed a crumpled wad of bills into his hand. "I want to have something to brag about at bingo."

"Ivy, could you come in here for a minute?" Her mother's voice wafted out the screen door onto the porch, where Ivy and Cade sat in the old wooden swing, too full of manicotti and meatballs to move. "Now."

"Uh, sure, Mom."

Cade gave her a sideways glance, eyebrows raised. "What did you do this time? Put syrup in the soap dispenser?"

"Not since high school. But I'm on her black list for some reason. I wonder if it has anything to do with all the phone calls." Her parents' landline had been ringing off the hook since dinner.

She'd barely finished speaking when it rang again. "See what I mean? I'd better go find out what's going on before the you-know-what hits the you-know-where."

"If it hasn't already."

"Thanks for the support."

"I do what I can."

"Wanna come with?" She stood and straightened her shirt.

"Thanks, but no thanks." He looked at his watch. "I'll go check on your dad. He's been out in the greenhouse for a while—probably to escape the telephone."

"Chicken."

"You got that right." Cade rose gingerly, still favoring his injured leg. "I'll take your father's orchids over your mom's outrage anytime."

She watched him cross the yard, appreciating the way his shorts pulled tight across his ass and how the muscles in his thighs, like steel cables, contracted and relaxed as he walked. Even with one leg encased in plastic, the man was lethally sexy.

"Ivy," her mom called again, her voice tinged with impatience.

"Coming."

She found her mother in the kitchen, still on the phone.

"I understand the board's concerns, Mr. Whitledge, and I'll speak to my daughter." She motioned for Ivy to sit. "I'm sure she was only thinking about the children and the new computers they so desperately need."

Ivy slumped into the high-backed kitchen chair, dread rolling over her like a cold, damp fog.

"Yes, I realize that's no excuse," her mother continued. "But I'd hardly call it pornography."

Pornography? What had she stepped in this time?

"No, I wouldn't call it public indecency, either. I'd call it a politically correct overreaction to what was clearly intended as a little harmless fun for a good cause. And I'd appreciate it if you called off your dogs. My husband is recovering from a heart attack, and these constant phone calls certainly aren't helping any."

Ivy's mother slammed the phone down and pulled the plug out of the wall. "*Stupido*. That'll show him."

"Ma." Ivy drummed her fingers on the table. "What's going on?"

"Self-righteous *stronzi*, every last one of them."

"Ma. Please."

"I'm sorry, *topolina*." Her mother pulled out a chair across from her and sat, wiping her hands on her apron.

"I repeat—" Ivy rested her chin on her hands and stared at her mother, trying to emulate her lawyer brother's cross-examination glare "—what's going on?"

"The board of education. *Stronzi!*" She started spewing Italian faster than Ivy could understand.

"I get it, Ma." Ivy cut her off. "They're assholes. That's a pretty strong word for you, and you've used it twice in the past minute. You're scaring me."

"They're a bunch of prudes. You and Cade raised twice as much money as any other booth. So what if he took off his shirt?"

"Is that what they're upset about?"

"Apparently they got a few complaints."

"A few?" Ivy sat straight up, her foot tapping a nervous tattoo on the tile floor. "From who?"

Her mother shifted in her chair. "They wouldn't say."

"So all those phone calls were from the board of ed?"

"Not exactly." Her mother avoided her gaze, pretending a sudden fascination in a string hanging from her apron. "We've gotten some complaints directly, too."

The tapping ended in a stomp. "You mean people are calling you to bitch about me?"

"Ivy. Language."

"For Christ's sake, Ma. You just called the board of ed assholes. Twice."

"That's different."

"Saying it in Italian doesn't make it any more acceptable, you know."

"Everything sounds nicer in Italian."

"What a nightmare." Ivy buried her head in her hands. "I knew this would happen if I came home."

"Knew what would happen?"

"Knew they'd find some reason to go after me."

"They?"

"This town. Everyone." Ivy groaned and dropped her head onto her forearms. "It's like high school all over again."

Her mother reached across the table and put a hand on her arm. "Was it that bad, *topolina*?"

"Worse." She hadn't told her parents the half of what some of the other kids did. Calling her names. Tripping her in the hall. Pushing her down the stairs. Stealing her books.

But she wasn't Jabba the Mutt anymore. No, now she was a pornographer. A pervert. A purveyor of smut.

The hand on Ivy's arm squeezed. Tight. "You are not a purveyor of smut."

Damn. She hadn't realized she'd said it out loud.

"Isn't that what all the callers said?"

"Not all." The hand withdrew. "I'd say it was about sixty-forty."

Ivy raised her head. "For me or against?"

"Against."

"I'm surprised I got forty percent."

"Maude can be pretty persuasive."

Ivy blew out a long, tortured sigh. "I should never

have come back. I don't belong here. I've never belonged here."

"How can you say that?" Ivy's father was standing in the doorway, his expression hard, an equally stern-faced Cade behind him. "You're family. Of course you belong here."

Open mouth, insert foot.

"I'm sorry. I didn't mean that I didn't belong with you guys. It's just this place." She looked around the kitchen, taking in everyone's stony faces. "Well, not this place. I mean…"

Ugh. She was babbling. Again.

Cade looked from Ivy to her mother and back again. "What's going on?"

"Nothing." Ivy shot her mother a warning glare, which was totally ignored. Instead, her mother proceeded to tell the entire sordid tale, complete with liberal use of the word *stronzi* and a whole host of other Italian profanities.

When it was over, Cade rolled his eyes. "Your mother's right. They're idiots. You can't let a handful of old dudes stuck in the 1960s run you out of town."

"Easy for you to say." Ivy huffed a stray lock of hair off her forehead. "You're Stockton's golden boy. Why do you think your phone's not blowing up even though you were the one with your shirt off?"

Cade leaned against the doorjamb and crossed his arms. "Good thing it *was* me. Just imagine the trouble we'd be in if you went topless."

"Not funny," Ivy grumbled, eyeing her father, who, surprisingly, appeared to be fighting off a smile under the thick, white beard he refused to shave even in the summer.

"It's a little funny." Her father lost the battle, the corners of his mouth curling upward.

"But the nursery—"

"Has been here for almost fifty years," her father interrupted. "God willing, it will be here for fifty more."

"What if people boycott? All those phone calls—"

"Were from a few disgruntled…" Her father looked to Ivy, his brows knotted. "What did your mother call them?"

"Stronzi," Cade, Ivy and her mother said in unison.

Ivy's father nodded. "That's it. *Stronzi*. No one with half a brain thinks what you and Cade did was inappropriate."

"Including you?" Ivy's eyes darted from her mother to her father.

"Of course, including us." Her mother's soft eyes widened. "Why would you think otherwise?"

"I don't know." Ivy stared at her Chuck Taylors. "You've never really said how you felt about my work. Some of my stuff is sort of…racy."

She winced, thinking of the swimsuit models she'd shot with dangerously low-slung bikini bottoms. Or that *Vanity Fair* cover of a very pregnant—and very naked— movie star. And the parade of shirtless men she'd photographed for high fashion ads…

"Your mother and I are nothing but proud of you, *min kära flicka*." Her father came and stood behind his wife, putting a hand on her shoulder. "You've built an entire career from the ground up, just like we built this nursery."

"We just wish you'd come home more often." Her mother reached back to cover her husband's hand with hers. "We miss you."

"I miss you guys, too." Ivy blinked back a tear. For the first time, the fallout of her lengthy absence hit her full force. Staying away from Stockton had kept the bad memories at bay. But it had kept her family at arm's length, too. Something she needed to change ASAP. Her parents weren't getting any younger, something her father's heart attack had driven home. Hard. "And I promise I'll visit at least once a month after I leave. Even if it's only for a day or two."

"That would be nice." Her mother sighed, her warm, brown eyes as watery as Ivy's. "I'm sure your brother and sisters would appreciate seeing more of you. And you've got a baby niece to consider now."

"Among others."

Ivy had almost forgotten Cade was there until he spoke up, still lounging in the doorway, a panty-moistening grin splitting his face. Her pulse went from trot to gallop, and heat spread up her neck to her face.

"It's late," she said, ducking her head to avoid her mother's all-seeing, all-knowing gaze. "We should get going."

"Thanks for dinner, Mr. and Mrs. Nelson." Cade pushed off the door frame and held out his hand to her father, who enveloped him in a bear hug instead.

"How many times have we asked you to call us Nils and Elena?" Her mother stood, opening her arms for her hug.

"Every other week since I graduated high school," Cade said, returning her embrace. "But old habits are hard to break."

They sure are, Ivy thought as she hugged her parents, said her goodbyes and followed the man she'd loved for as long as she could remember to her car.

15

"I CAN'T TIE this damn thing." Cade frowned at his reflection in the mirror. "And I don't see why I have to wear a monkey suit in the first place."

He swore under his breath and pulled both ends of the bow tie, unraveling it for what was probably his tenth attempt to get it right. He could wake from a dead sleep and have his PPE on in seconds, but give him a harmless little piece of silk and he was all thumbs. He adjusted the ends so one was longer than the other and started over. Cross the long over the short, bring it up through the loop, double up the short end...

"Technically, you don't. But I never could resist a man in a tux."

He looked from his reflection to Ivy's and gave up on the tie. The sleeveless navy dress she wore was simple, but it hugged her curves like a Lamborghini on a switchback, ending midthigh and showing off a decent expanse of her shapely legs.

"Need some help?" she asked, taking him by the shoulders and spinning him around to face her.

"Wow, that dress..." His gaze roamed from her long

neck, over the lush mounds of her breasts, down her smooth legs and back up again, and he swallowed hard. "You look stunning."

"Thanks." She finished off his tie with a flourish and stood back to admire her handiwork. "You clean up pretty good yourself."

"So whose wedding is this anyway?"

"The niece of some bigwig on the school board. I'm doing it gratis to smooth things over from the whole carnival fiasco. Practically the entire town's going to be there, including Maude and her cronies. So prepare to have your ass pinched. A lot. But try to keep your shirt on."

He sat on the bed and reached for one of the black oxfords he'd borrowed from Gabe for the occasion. He'd drawn the line at the shiny patent-leather shoes the guy at the tuxedo rental place had tried to sell him on. Bad enough he was still in the walking cast. He wasn't about to make himself even more uncomfortable by stuffing his one good foot into something stiff, squeaky and rented. "I'm your assistant. Aren't you're supposed to protect me?"

"I'll be too busy working." Ivy checked her lipstick in the mirror, rubbing a smudge of coral off her teeth. "Besides, you're a big boy. You can stand up for yourself. Or are you scared of a bunch of senior citizens?"

"They may be old, but they're feisty. And they travel in packs. Like wolves." He double-knotted his shoelaces and shuddered. "Really horny wolves."

She turned from the mirror and smoothed down the front of her dress. "My money's on you. Ready to go?"

He tightened his brace under the leg of his tuxedo pants and stood. "As I'll ever be."

They grabbed her gear and loaded it in the used Honda Element she'd picked up when she'd gotten tired of pulling up to gigs in her father's ancient pickup with the Grower's Paradise logo emblazoned on the side. Cade dealt with the bulky tripod and light stands and Ivy handled the bag with the more delicate cameras and lenses. It was a routine that had become familiar in the two weeks since he'd first accompanied her to the carnival.

She still spent mornings at the nursery, waking up at 5:00 a.m. to make sure everything was stocked, tagged, trimmed and watered. Then they opened for business at nine and her mother took over. Cade had offered to help out there, too, but she'd flatly refused, saying it was bad enough he'd gotten sucked into indentured servitude as her photographer's assistant. They'd done a number of portraits and parties together—sometimes two gigs a day—and he'd become pretty damn good at it. Like a top-notch golf caddy, he'd learned to anticipate his boss's needs, handing Ivy the right flash before she could ask for it, or a memory card just as the one she was using filled up.

He hadn't minded helping out. He figured the work would bring them closer together. Instead, it seemed to drive an emotional wedge between them—a wedge at least partly of his own making. The more he watched Ivy work, the more one simple, inescapable thought took hold in his brain and wouldn't let go.

Ivy was right. She didn't belong in Stockton. She was meant for bigger, better things. And he'd be a selfish bastard if he asked her to stay.

So he'd started pulling back, preparing himself for the time in the not so distant future when she'd pack her bags and hit the road. He'd begun stopping by the station every other day for an hour or two and hanging out with the guys a couple of nights a week. He would move back to his own apartment, just as soon as his doctor gave him the thumbs-up on climbing the stairs.

Not that he'd shared that last part of the plan with Ivy. Yet.

"Where to?" he asked when they were in the car and she'd started to back down the driveway.

"The first stop is just down the street."

"First stop?"

"Yep. The waterfall at the other end of Leffert's Pond."

"Isn't that the place where everyone went for pictures before the prom?"

"I wouldn't know." She looked both ways, her eyes somehow managing to skip right over him in the passenger seat, and eased the car out onto the road. "I didn't go to prom. No one asked me."

Way to go, Hardesty. Remind her how miserable she was here. That'll make her run away even faster.

He shrugged and stared at the scenery rushing by outside the car window, doing his best to downplay his case of foot-in-mouth syndrome. "You didn't miss much."

"That's not what I heard." She flashed him an I-know-something-you-don't-know grin before turning her attention back to the road. "I heard a certain quarterback and a certain cheerleader were caught with their pants down, so to speak, in the stairwell."

"Those rumors were greatly exaggerated." He smiled back at her. "We were only making out. And we were fully clothed at all times."

"There's a lot you can do with your clothes on." The tips of her ears flushed an adorable bright pink. "So I'm told."

"Telling is good. Showing is better." His gaze traveled south from her face, stopping at her legs. Cade was mesmerized by the play of the muscles in her nylon-clad thigh as her foot moved from the gas pedal to the brake. He shifted in his seat to relieve the growing pressure against his zipper.

"Are you offering?" she asked playfully, still concentrating on her driving and blissfully unaware of his condition.

He didn't have a chance to answer before she pulled into the parking lot beside a small waterfall. The smallest natural falls in the country, if you believed the hype from the Stockton parks and recreation department. The town even honored the darned thing with a festival every fall.

A wooden footbridge spanned the top of the waterfall, and a picnic area, with several tables and a barbecue pit, was situated at the base. The bride, easily identifiable in her white gown, hovered near one of the tables, surrounded by a group of formally dressed men and women Cade presumed made up the wedding party. Why else would seven women be wearing the same ugly-ass orange dress?

"You must be Ivy." A woman in a crisp, light gray pantsuit broke free from the crowd and approached them almost before they could get out of the car. "I'm the mother of the bride. There's a few things I'd like to discuss with you before we get started."

She took Ivy by the elbow and spirited her off, leaving Cade to grapple with the equipment.

"So it's true." A familiar singsongy voice made him jump, and he almost banged his head on the open hatchback.

"Sasha." He withdrew from the car, a tripod in one

hand and Ivy's camera bag in the other. He slammed the hatch shut, hitched the bag over his shoulder and faced her.

"It's true," she repeated, shaking her head. "You're her lackey."

"I'm helping a friend."

"Friend?" She took a step toward him, her perfectly plucked eyebrows arched. "My sources say you two are shacking up."

Her sources? Who did she think she was, Katie freaking Couric? He tucked the tripod under his arm and studied her. Even an in-your-face sexpot like Sasha couldn't make that hideous dress look good. "What if we are?"

"You can do better, you know." She put a hand on his forearm.

He shook it off. "If by better you mean you, I'll pass."

Cade looked around for Ivy. He found her above him on the footbridge with Momzilla, who was gesturing wildly. She was pointing at something or someone down below, and Ivy's head turned in the same direction. He could tell by the way she stiffened the moment her eyes landed on him and Sasha.

"Duty calls." He tightened his grip on the strap of the camera bag, backed away from his ex and eyed the steep, wooden stairway that wound up the side of the falls. Doctor be damned, he was going up there. He had to reach Ivy before the wrong impression was cemented firmly in her mind.

"Have a nice time at the wedding," he said over his shoulder as he navigated around the picnic tables toward the steps. "Good luck catching the bouquet."

If she did, one thing was for sure. He was staying the hell away from the garter.

"Perfect." Ivy crouched down to get a better angle of the wedding party lined up on the footbridge. "One more for good luck and we're all done here."

And not a moment too soon. The higher the sun got, the more the bride was starting to spritz, and a sweaty bride did not for good photos make.

Then there was the added bonus of putting as much distance as possible between herself and Sasha. Once the posed prewedding photos were done, all that was left were the candids at the church and reception. It would be easier to avoid the evil eye Cade's ex was shooting her in a crowd.

If she was still his ex. Ivy shrugged off the surge of what she knew was irrational jealousy. So he'd been talking to Sasha. So what? What was he supposed to do, ignore her when she came right up to him? Take her down with a karate chop to the back of the head? Anyway, it was Ivy's house he was living in, Ivy's bed he was sleeping in at night. Well, technically her sister's house and her sister's bed. But it was Ivy he was sharing them with.

"That's a wrap." She snapped the lens cap on her camera and stood slowly, thanks to her short skirt. "Thanks, everyone. I'll see you all over at the church."

She moved to one side, letting the members of the wedding party pass her on the narrow path from the bridge to the stairs. Only one—Sasha, natch—seemed to find it impossible to get by without elbowing her in the ribs, almost making her drop her Nikon.

"Sorry about that," Cade said as he came up beside her, camera bag over one arm and tripod in the other.

"Why?" Ivy handed him the camera, which he stowed carefully in the bag. "You didn't do anything."

"I should never have agreed to the whole fake date thing in the first place. Then Sasha wouldn't have it in for you."

Yeah. And they would never have wound up sleeping together. Was he regretting that, too?

Ivy pushed aside that pesky thought and took the camera bag from Cade. "I don't know. I'm pretty sure she'd find some other reason to hate me."

Girls like her usually did.

With a sigh so low not even whales could hear it, Ivy started down the path toward the stairway.

"Do you need a hand?" she asked, suddenly wondering how he'd gotten up there in the first place. She'd been so occupied with the controlling mother of the bride she hadn't even thought about how he'd gotten to her side. "I can take the tripod…"

"Nah." He waved her off. "I'm right behind you."

When she reached the bottom, she turned. *Right behind* was apparently a relative term, as Cade was still making his way down, moving slowly, his free hand clutching the rail with every step, but managing pretty well despite the extra encumbrances of his cast and the tripod.

Ivy's heart did a nosedive to her stomach. If he could climb up and down the precarious staircase at the falls, he could certainly manage the one at his apartment, and that meant he could go home. Something that had probably occurred to him, too.

"Let's roll," he said when he reached her, putting a hand at the small of her back like she was the walking wounded and not the other way around. "We don't want to be late for the ceremony."

Just as Ivy predicted, avoiding Sasha's stink eye was

easier at the church and even simpler at the reception, with everyone busy dining and dancing. As a photographer, Ivy's favorite part of any wedding was the reception. Sure, the ceremony was beautiful. And there was nothing quite like the expression on a groom's face when he saw his bride walk down the aisle.

But what she liked capturing best were the unscripted, unexpected moments. The groom's head thrown back in laughter at some questionable joke in the best man's toast. The tear running down the father of the bride's face when he danced with his daughter. The subtle, longing glances between the bride and groom when no one else was paying attention.

Would anyone ever look at her like that? Would Cade?

"You've got plenty of pictures." The man at the center of her thoughts took the camera from her hand and set it down on a nearby table. "Dance with me."

He held out a palm. She looked from it to her expensive camera and back again.

"My Nikon…"

"Will be fine." He pulled out his wallet, extracted a five-dollar bill and waved it in front of a floppy-haired boy of about thirteen who was sitting at the table, engrossed in a video game on his phone. "Keep an eye on this for me, okay? There's five more in it for you when we come back."

The boy blew his bangs off his forehead and looked up from the game. "Make it ten up front and ten more on the flip side, and you've got a deal."

Cade pulled out another five and plunked it on the table. "Fine."

Without waiting for any sort of acknowledgment from

Ivy, he took her by the hand and led her onto the dance floor.

"You got robbed," she said.

"I'll be the judge of that."

The band chose that moment to slow things down, launching into Chris de Burgh's "The Lady in Red." Ivy's heart fluttered as Cade drew her flush against him. The heat from his body surrounded her and the scent of his skin, mossy and heady from his cologne, mingled with the sweet smell of the flowers in the elaborate table centerpieces.

"It bought me a dance with you," he continued as if she wasn't about to dissolve into a puddle of love right there on the dance floor. "That's money well spent in my book."

She tore her gaze from the strong, tanned column of his throat and locked eyes with the mother of the bride, who pursed her lips and whispered something in her husband's ear. "I'm on the clock. I really shouldn't be…"

"Shh." Cade shushed her with a finger on her lips. "Relax. Enjoy yourself. One dance, then you can go back to being Margaret Bourke-White."

Ivy tipped her head to stare up at him incredulously. The female photographer, known for her war correspondence and *Life* magazine covers, wasn't exactly a household name. "You know Margaret Bourke-White?"

"Not personally." His smile was broad but forced, and it didn't come close to reaching his eyes. She couldn't see that special light they got when his pleasure was genuine. "But I'm familiar with her work. I might not be a Rhodes Scholar like my parents, but I'm not living under a rock. And I do read."

"I didn't mean to imply that you're stupid." She

reached up to caress his cheek and realized that they'd stopped moving. "I don't believe that. I never have. And I never will."

"I know. Hell, you're the one who encouraged me to take the lieutenant exam." He turned his head to kiss her palm. "Just a sore spot, I guess. I'm sorry."

"Don't be." She slid her hand along his stubbled jaw, down his neck to his shoulder. "Now are you going to dance with me or just stand there? From the look on Momzilla's face, I'd say we've got three minutes max before she storms over here, rips us apart and reads me the riot act for ruining her precious baby's special day."

"Then by all means, let's dance."

His arms tightened around her, and they swayed together in silence for the rest of the song. As they danced, every inch of her body became more and more aware of every inch of his. Especially the rock-hard inches pressing against her thigh.

When the song ended, the lead singer swung his guitar around to his back and gripped the microphone. "Okay, folks, we're gonna take a little break while the staff gets everything set up for the cake. Be back in fifteen."

Reluctantly, Ivy stepped out of Cade's arms and clapped politely along with the rest of the crowd. "I need to use the little girls' room before they cut the cake. Can you rescue my camera from the teenage extortionist you entrusted it to?"

"Sure."

She started to kiss his cheek but froze midpucker when she saw the mother of the bride bearing down on them. Instead, she settled for a quick squeeze of his manly forearm, bare now that he'd shed his tux jacket and rolled up his shirtsleeves. Who knew forearms could be so sexy? Corded and sprinkled with just the right amount of soft, fair hair. Biceps had nothing on them. "Gotta run. Meet me over by the cake table, okay? And bring the camera bag. I want to swap lenses."

She hurried to the restroom before the festivities started up again. She was washing her hands, remembering the feel of Cade's sculpted back muscles under her palms as they swayed in time with the music, when the door swung open and Sasha tottered in, more than a little unsteady on her four-inch heels and reeking of cheap beer.

"Hiding out in the bathroom?" Sasha stumbled to the sink next to Ivy, leaning heavily on it for balance. "Shouldn't you be working?"

Ivy dried her hands on a paper towel and tossed it into the wastebasket. "I was just on my way out."

"It won't last, you know." Sasha fumbled through her clutch, finally pulling out a lipstick.

Ivy stared at her. "Excuse me?"

"This thing you've got going with Cade. I give it two months, tops." Sasha uncapped the lipstick and rolled it up to reveal a shade of do-me red. No surprise there. "And if my math's right, it's close to that now."

"I don't see how it's any of your business."

"What he needs is someone like me." Sasha leaned in to the mirror for a closer look and ran the cherry-red gloss over her lips, smacking them together when she was done. She was amazingly proficient for someone who'd clearly had a few too many. Probably due to years of experience applying makeup while shitfaced.

"Someone pretty and put-together, who'll be happy staying with him here in Stockton," she rambled on, not even bothering to spare a glance at Ivy. "Not a fat, frumpy photographer who's made no secret of how much she hates this place."

It's not the place I hate. It's people like you. Ivy clutched the edge of the sink basin in front of her to prevent herself from committing any number of crimes involving serious bodily injury that her brother, Mr. Law-and-Order, would be first in line to prosecute her for. She could pretend all she wanted, but even after twelve years, six continents and countless lectures from her mentor-turned-business-partner Andre, fat shaming still stung.

"I think that's for Cade to decide, not you. Maybe he prefers a woman with curves to a stick figure."

"Oh, please." Sasha capped the lipstick and stowed it back in her purse. "He's a man. What does he know? What do any of them know? It's up to us to show them what's good for them."

"Sexist, much?" Ivy asked, rolling her eyes.

"It's not sexist if it's true." Sasha stepped back, surveyed the results in the mirror and smiled. "There. That ought to do it."

She turned her critical gaze on Ivy, scrutinizing her from head to toe, her eyes narrowing as they traveled over the lumps and bumps Ivy's dress did nothing to conceal. "You should really consider liposuction. Or that surgery where they staple your stomach shut. I've heard it works wonders."

Ivy's grip on the sink went from firm to white-knuckled. "Thanks, but no thanks."

"Your loss. Or not." Sasha chuckled at her own bad joke, then pushed past Ivy and lurched unsteadily for the door. At the last second, she turned back with a knowing smile that dripped contempt. "But you might want to at least fix your dress. The skirt's tucked into the top of your panty hose."

16

IVY WAS CLICKING through the wedding photos on her laptop at the kitchen counter a few days later. She was weeding out the wheat from the chaff before she uploaded the good ones to Dropbox for the bride—and her mother, Ivy was sure—when her cell rang. The overseas number was familiar, and it gave rise to a mix of anticipation and dread.

"Now, Andre," she half teased without preamble. "I told you I'd call you when I was ready to come back to work."

"But *ma mie*," he said in his lilting French accent, his voice a touch wounded. "What I have for you is the opportunity of a lifetime."

The corners of her mouth curved into a smile, both at the nickname—what was it with her and all the foreign nicknames? Her mother. Her father. Andre—and the overexaggeration. According to Andre, every opportunity was once-in-a-lifetime. "What is it this time? The cover of Italian *Vogue*? A week shooting another famous model in the Turks and Caicos?"

"Bah," he scoffed, his disdain evident even thousands of miles away over the phone. She could just imagine him waving a well-manicured hand in annoyance. "You've been there and done that. This is the celebrity wedding of the year. Maybe even the decade. And they want you to have exclusive access. No competition. No assistants. Just you."

Great. Another wedding. Except for this one she'd probably have to fly halfway across the globe to do the same thing she'd done not seventy-two hours ago practically in her own backyard. And she wouldn't have Cade backing her up. What might have been tempting a few months ago suddenly didn't seem all the appealing. "Can't you do it?"

"Sadly, *non*. The bride wants you and you only. You shot her last year for *Marie Claire*."

He named a model whose on-again, off-again relationship with a certain rock star had been tabloid fodder for months.

Ivy gave a low whistle. "Damn. Those photos will go for a pretty penny."

"And then some," Andre agreed. "Precisely why you can't say no."

I can and I will, Ivy thought. Sure, the money was good. But she had money. She'd made plenty over the past few years and invested it wisely with Gabe's help, giving her a nice little nest egg.

What she didn't have—and desperately wanted—was more time with Cade. He hadn't said a word about moving out, but seeing the way he'd handled those stairs at the waterfall she knew that was high on the list of coming attractions. And then there was Sasha's warning. As much as Ivy hated to admit it, she had a point. Ivy had known going in that this relationship had an expiration date. She just didn't want it to be over quite yet.

Or—truth be told—ever.

"Can I think about it?" she asked, stalling for time.

"Bien." She could almost hear him removing his wire-rimmed glasses and pinching the bridge of his nose. "But think fast. She needs an answer by the end of the week. The wedding's the weekend after Labor Day at some private estate in Belize."

Ivy checked the magnetic calendar on the refrigerator. Today was Tuesday. That gave her four days to come up with a game plan. "No problem. I'll call you before then and let you know."

"Make sure you do," Andre scolded, sounding like he was the parent and she a reluctant teenager. "It's the—"

"I know, I know," she interrupted, laughing. "The opportunity of a lifetime. *À bientôt, mon cher.*"

"What's the opportunity of a lifetime?"

Cade's voice made her jump as she ended the call, just managing to fumble her cell onto the counter next to her laptop as it slipped out of her startled fingers. She turned around to find him in the doorway between the kitchen and the dining room, his feet spread apart like a prizefighter, one hand gripping each side of the doorjamb. Her heart swelled at the sight of him and she held on to the lip of the granite countertop behind her for support. If she ignored the cast on his leg, he looked like a fitness model in his tank top and athletic shorts, the finely developed muscles of his upper arms on full display. And then there were those damn forearms…

"It's nothing." She waved her hand dismissively like she imagined Andre had done only seconds earlier. "Andre thinks every opportunity is a life-changing event."

"Your boss?" He shoved off the door frame and strode into the room, leaning against the counter next to her and overwhelming her with his closeness.

She slid a smidge to the side, needing a little breathing room for sheer self-preservation. "More like partner, but yeah."

"So what is it this time?"

"Some celebrity wedding."

"Can I come?" He did that brow-waggling thing he did when he was trying to be suggestive. "I'm good at weddings."

"One wedding and now you're an expert?"

"Hey, I fended off Maude and her randy band of geriatrics. In a cast. I'd say that qualifies me for the big time."

"It does, but I'm not going. And even if I was, the answer would be no. This one's top secret. They haven't even announced their engagement." She turned back to her laptop and started scrolling through the pictures again, hoping it would put an end to the conversation.

"What do you mean you're not going?" He reached over and gently closed her laptop. "If it's as secret as all that, those pictures will be worth a fortune."

She faced him, arms crossed in front of her chest. "You sound like Andre."

"Is that good or bad?"

"He's sixty-five years old, wears plaids with stripes, but somehow manages to pull it off, and treats me like a petulant child." She shrugged. "You be the judge."

"Not exactly what I was going for."

The alarm on her phone went off, telling her it was

five o'clock. Time to text her dad and make sure he took his meds with dinner. Her thumbs flew on the keypad as she talked. "You're home early. Weren't you supposed to go to the Half Pint with the guys tonight?"

"Change of plans." He plucked the phone out of her hand and set it on the counter. "And nice try, switching subjects. But you're not getting off that easy. We're discussing your schedule, not mine. Specifically your upcoming trip to...where did you say this shindig was?"

"I didn't." She squinted up at him. "Trying to get rid of me?"

"Hardly." He braced a hand on the granite on either side of her, trapping her between the counter and his hard, hot body. "But it's just a couple of days, right? Your dad's well on his way to a full recovery. The new staff at the nursery can pick up the slack. And I'll be fine on my own for a little while."

No, it wasn't just a couple of days. If she said yes to this, she'd be saying yes to going back to her old life. She'd have no excuse when Andre called again. And he would call again. And again. And again. But she didn't know how to explain that to Cade without revealing that he was the reason she wanted to stay. Sasha's words of warning echoed in her head. *It won't last.* So she stuck with the safe, if completely untrue, approach.

"Trust me, it's no big deal. Andre's a huge drama queen. We get offers like this all the time and turn most of them down. We even said no to George and Amal." She crossed her fingers behind her back and prayed some higher power wouldn't strike her down for lying.

"Seriously?"

She nodded, afraid to tempt fate by voicing the lie again.

He frowned. "You're going to have to go back to work eventually, you know."

Did she?

"I am working." She reached behind her and patted her laptop. "We have the Levenson bar mitzvah this weekend. And a pet portrait tomorrow."

Cade shook his head. "That stuff is small potatoes."

"Not to the Levensons. Or Mrs. Thorpe and her Chihuahua."

"You know what I mean." He took a step back and ran a hand through his spiky blond hair. "There's a big difference between photographing celebrities and taking pictures of a barking, hairless rat."

Yeah. The dog is a thousand times better behaved, she thought. *And knows how to follow directions.* "Maybe I like small potatoes."

"No one likes small potatoes."

"Please." She put a hand on one of those manly forearms she loved so much. The fine, golden hairs teased her palm. "Trust me on this. I'll know when it's time to go."

If that time ever comes. And it won't, if you ask me to stay.

Ask me to stay.

Her Jedi mind powers must have deserted her because Cade ignored her silent plea. "Okay. I'll trust you. For now."

"Thanks." She rose up on her toes and bussed his cheek, his sexy stubble tickling her lips.

He turned his head and captured her mouth in a searing kiss that left her breathless. "Wanna go get something to eat?"

Leave it to a man to think of food after a kiss like that.

"How about we stay in tonight instead?" Ivy asked when she'd regained her composure and could put words in a meaningful order. "My mom sent over a lasagna."

Good thing. Ivy's own cooking skills were sorely lacking. It wasn't like she had much chance to practice on the road, hence her burning of the pasta and the resulting need to be rescued from the indignity of the doggy door. Cade had it all over her in the chef department, thanks to his years of practice at the firehouse.

"And after dinner?" He circled his arms around her, pulling her close.

She melted into his embrace.

"Why, dessert, of course." That much she could handle, with a little help from the Rolling Pin.

"Cream puffs?" he asked, reading her mind. Sure, when it came to sex he could tell what she was thinking.

"I thought we could finish what we started when we were so rudely interrupted all those weeks ago."

"Do you have the blindfold?" His voice was a low, husky growl filled with raw, animal need that made her shiver with answering desire.

She nodded and blushed, suddenly unsure of herself, something she usually wasn't with Cade. But this, what she wanted to ask him…was it too much? Would he resist? Sometimes what was good for the goose wasn't good for the gander. She took a deep, shuddering breath and plunged full steam ahead. "I thought…maybe…you could wear it this time."

He bent his head to whisper in her ear. "As you wish."

CADE PADDED TO the kitchen for a glass of water. Damn, the woman was unpredictable. And inventive. And exhausting. No doubt when she woke up she'd be ready for another round. Was it three? Or four? He'd lost count. Whatever round it was, it wasn't going to happen unless he got some hydration.

He grabbed a glass out of the cupboard next to the sink and shuffled to the refrigerator, catching a glimpse of his naked form in the stainless steel and smiling. He liked not having to worry about wearing his brace—or anything else—at night. Liked knowing that the only person who could catch him wandering around in the buff was Ivy. Liked imagining what would happen if she did.

Liked her.

Loved her.

He'd stopped fighting his feelings, given up his idiotic plan to put some distance between himself and Ivy. Time was their enemy, and he wasn't going to rob them of any more of it. That was why he'd blown off the gang at the Half Pint. The thought of another night apart, when for all he knew she'd be on a plane to who knows where tomorrow, made him literally sick to his stomach.

And what a night it had been. Cold cream puffs and hot sex with Ivy beat darts and watered-down beer with Sykes and Hansen any night of the week.

Cade poured himself a glass of water from the dispenser on the refrigerator, sucked it down and poured another. He leaned against the counter as he drank, watching dust specks dancing in the moonlight that filtered in through the window above the sink.

The night had been perfect in every way—save one. Cade couldn't shake the feeling Ivy wasn't being entirely truthful about the whole celebrity-wedding thing. It sounded like a bigger deal than she was making it out to be. And that meant this Andre guy was right, and she was passing up the chance of a lifetime.

Why? For her father? For him? Would she really choose him over her career? Would he want her to?

Out of the corner of his eye he caught the bright pink case of her cell phone on the other end of the counter, mocking him. He knew her pass code. They'd exchanged them one night in a raunchy, two-person game of strip truth or dare. It would be easy for him to locate Andre's number, call him and find out what was really going on.

But he'd promised to trust her. And as much as he doubted her story about George and Amal and celebrity weddings being just another gig, he intended to keep his promises to her.

With a groan, he polished off his water, put the glass in the sink and headed back to the bedroom.

Cade was still reminding himself of his promise to trust Ivy the next morning when the house phone rang. He answered it and was met with a barrage of rapid-fire French. At least, he thought it was French. In the midst of the tirade, he caught Ivy's name and the words *sérieux* and *pressant*.

"I'm sorry," he blurted when the caller paused to take a breath. "But Ivy's not home right now. This is her…"

What was he? Her live-in lover? Her boy toy? He settled on the annoyingly generic.

"This is her friend Cade."

"Ah-h-h-h." The caller drew the word out like he was savoring it, rolling it over his tongue to see how it tasted. "Now I understand her reluctance to leave Stockton and all its…charms."

"Can I give her a message?" Cade asked, choosing

to ignore the obvious implication and taking up the pad and pen Ivy kept by the phone.

"Please. She is not answering her cell."

"She's at the nursery. Reception's spotty." Plus, it was hard to take a phone call when you were shoveling shit.

"Tell her Andre called. There's been a change of plan. The wedding's been moved up two weeks, to the weekend before Labor Day. Something about needing to stay one step ahead of the gossip magazines. Anyway, the bride needs an answer by the end of business today, your time."

Now it was Cade's turn.

"Ah. So you're Andre? Can I ask you something?"

"Will you give her the message?"

"Of course."

"Then ask away."

Cade hesitated, knowing once he started there was no turning back. "This wedding...it's a big deal?"

"Mais oui." Andre's voice was emphatic. *"C'est une très grande affaire.* Or, as you Americans say, a very big deal. It is not every day one gets offered exclusive rights to an event like this one. It could open all sorts of doors for Ivy."

Busted.

"Thanks, Andre. I'll give her the message as soon as she gets in, which should be—" he looked at the clock on the stove...8:05 a.m. "—in about an hour."

"Merci to you, too, *mon ami.* Take good care of our Ivy."

Our Ivy.

But only Cade's on loan. And the lease had just expired.

He hung up the phone with a click that echoed in the

quiet kitchen. Hard as it was, he knew what he had to do. It would be easier this way, for him and for her. A clean break, quick and relatively painless, like ripping off a Band-Aid.

Except it wouldn't be painless. Not for him.

Still, he had to go. He'd been ready to move back to his apartment for almost a week, and they both knew it. And if he didn't leave, Ivy would miss this big opportunity. She might be okay with that now, but what about in ten years? Or twenty, when she was still taking pictures of small-town brides and pampered pets? He didn't want that on his shoulders. No way. He'd had enough of that kind of resentment from his parents to last a lifetime.

He picked up the phone again and dialed.

"Brannigan," his buddy answered on the first ring.

"Can you come get me in half an hour?"

"At Ivy's?"

"Yep."

"The lady of the house too busy to chauffeur you around this morning?"

Damn. Cade was hoping Trey would be too tired or hung over to ask him many questions. "Something like that. I'll give you the details when you pick me up."

"Okay. See you in thirty."

His ride secured, Cade made his way to the guest room and started emptying out his belongings, pulling clothes from the dresser and the closet and shoving them in his duffel bag. When he was done, he threw in his toiletries from the adjoining bathroom on top of it all and zipped the whole thing up with five minutes to spare before Trey was due to arrive.

He used the time to write Ivy a note. He'd never been much of a wordsmith, but he couldn't leave without saying something. After a few false starts, he settled on short, simple and to the point. When he was done, he picked up his duffel bag and walked out the door without looking back.

17

"How are things with you and Cade?"

Noelle sat back and eyed Ivy from across the farmhouse table in their parents' kitchen, sipping her omnipresent herbal tea. She'd driven up for a short visit before flying out for a monthlong European tour. But with one of the part-timers working at the nursery that morning, their mother had announced she was taking their father for a much-needed haircut, giving the sisters a little bonding time before Ivy's session with Mrs. Thorpe's Chihuahua. And Noelle had apparently decided to use the opportunity to grill Ivy about her relationship status, or lack thereof.

"And don't bother denying there's a you-and-Cade," she said as Ivy opened her mouth to do just that. "Gabe told me he walked in on you two getting creative with cream puffs."

Ivy groaned and dropped her head into her hands. "Is nothing sacred?"

"Hell no." Noelle's answer was quick and decisive. "Not between siblings."

"He didn't say anything to Mom and Dad, did he?"

Ivy would kill him if he had. Even if it got her life in prison for murdering a prosecutor. She'd never be able to look her parents in the eye again. And they'd probably disown Cade, which would crush him. He was closer to them than he was to his own family. But she'd know by now if Gabe had blabbed to them, wouldn't she?

"No way. Can you even imagine that conversation?" Noelle shuddered in mock horror. "Besides, the full-disclosure rule only applies between brothers and sisters. So disclose."

"There's not much to say." Ivy dumped two packets of sweetener into her coffee, ignoring her sister's judgmental glare. Nothing the least bit processed ever went into her sister's perfect body. Not that Ivy was jealous. She saw the pressure Noelle and her ballerina friends lived under every day to keep off the pounds. She didn't have that kind of self-discipline and didn't want it. What good was life if you couldn't indulge once in a while? Like she was indulging with Cade. "He's staying at my place until he can manage the stairs at his apartment."

"And you're banging each other's brains out."

"I'm helping out a friend."

"A friend who's banging your brains out, and vice versa."

"It's a matter of convenience."

"Yeah, I'd say. Living together must make it pretty convenient for you to bang each other's brains out 24/7."

"Fine." Ivy slammed her cup down on the table, sloshing hot coffee on her hand. She yelped and dashed to the sink to run the burn under cold water, which also gave her a reason to turn her back to her sister, shielding her rapidly reddening face. "We're banging each other's brains out. Are you happy?"

"The question is, are *you* happy?"

Leave it to Noelle to get to the heart of the matter. Pun intended. She might be the baby of the family, but she was no slouch when it came to reading situations. Or people. She'd always been able to read Ivy like the Yellow Pages.

Ivy shut off the faucet and reached for a dishcloth to dry her hands. She drew it out as long as possible before turning back to Noelle.

"I am, and I'm not," she admitted, resting her butt against the counter.

"What's that mean?" Noelle frowned, creating a crease in her flawless forehead. "Is the sex bad? I can't imagine it is with a certified stud like Cade."

"Certified stud?" Ivy tossed the dishcloth onto the counter. "Who talks like that?"

"The corps de ballet." Noelle looked longingly at a box of Pepperidge Farm cookies their mother had left on the counter then shook her head as if to wipe it from her consciousness. "You're avoiding my question."

"About the sex?"

"Of course about the sex," Noelle huffed.

"The sex is…" This was awkward. What was she supposed to tell her baby sister? That sex with Cade was earth-shaking? Mind-blowing? Life-altering? "Fine."

"There's no such thing as 'fine' sex. If it's 'fine,' you're doing it wrong."

Oh, they weren't doing it wrong. As far as Ivy was concerned, if it got any more right she'd die of pure pleasure. "Okay, it's off the charts. Through the roof. Best I've ever had. Satisfied?"

"Sounds like you are. So what's the problem? Unless…" Noelle bit her lip.

Ivy took her seat again, leaning forward to rest her elbows on the table. "Unless what?"

"Unless you want more. Like a commitment. Forever. A house with garage, a Goldendoodle and enough kids to field your own Little League team. And you're not sure Cade's the guy to give it to you."

"You sound like you're speaking from experience." Ivy studied her sister carefully. Was Noelle thinking about settling down, too? Last Ivy had heard, she was dating some hotshot choreographer, but no one in the family had met him, despite their mother's efforts to get him to make the two-hour drive from New York to Stockton. From what Ivy had learned online, the guy was a real piece of work—the terror of the dance community, known for reducing everyone from the corps dancers to the principals to tears. Male and female both. She couldn't imagine what her sister saw in him.

"This is your intervention," Noelle insisted. "Not mine."

Ivy lifted her coffee cup to her lips but didn't drink, instead staring at her sister over the rim. "So it's an intervention now?"

"If that's what it takes."

"Takes for what?"

"For you to get off your ass and tell Cade you love him. That you're done globe-trotting and you're ready to put down roots here in Stockton, with him." Noelle reached across the table and covered Ivy's hand with her own. "You are, right?"

Ivy nodded, able to think the words but not say them.

She loved Cade. She'd always loved Cade. That much hadn't changed. What was different was her. She'd seen the world, found herself and made peace with her past.

Now she wanted to come back home and be with him and take pictures that made people feel good about themselves instead of inadequate and insecure. And maybe someday have that Little League team Noelle talked about.

"I knew it." Her sister rounded the table and pulled Ivy to her feet. "Then what are you doing here with me? Go get your man."

Less than five minutes later and with a fair amount of prodding from Noelle, Ivy was backing her Element down the driveway as her sister waved and shouted, "Call me later. Much later, if things go like I think they will."

Ivy had no idea what she was going to say to Cade. Or what his response would be. But one of them had to be brave enough to put their heart on the line. And in a way, she was perversely proud that person was going to be her and not the big, brawny prototypical hero fireman.

Who's the tough one now? she thought, smiling as she pulled into the street.

Ivy drove as fast as she dared to the lake house, cutting her normal travel time in half. Her father had always said that once she'd set her mind on something it was a done deal, and now that she'd set her mind on confessing her feelings to Cade she wanted the deal done as soon as possible. At least then she'd know the outcome and be able to navigate through the aftermath, good or bad.

The locked front door should have been her first tip-off that something was amiss. She shrugged it off, figuring maybe Cade was taking a shower and didn't want to risk any of his buddies walking in on him. Fishing her key out of her purse, she let herself in.

"I'm home," she called as she pushed the door open.

No answering shout. No noise from the TV or Pandora or any one of Cade's video games.

"Hello?" The door shut behind her, the snick of the latch reverberating in the eerie silence of the too-quiet house.

Sleeping. That must be it. After the night of acrobatic sex they'd had, she wasn't surprised he needed a little rest.

She tiptoed down the hall to the guest room, inching the door open so as not to wake him.

Empty.

Her palms were sweating now, panic starting to set in. Could he have gone out with his friends? He'd done that before when she was at work, but he'd always called or texted. She pulled out her phone and swiped the screen to make sure she hadn't missed anything.

No calls. No texts.

She dropped the phone back into her purse and raced from room to room, calling his name.

Nothing.

When she got to the kitchen, she saw it. The key she'd given him. It was hard to miss, on a Super Mario key chain she'd picked out just for him. Underneath it lay one of the sheets of paper from the notepad she kept by the phone, folded in half with her name scrawled along the top.

She slid Mario to the side and picked up the paper. She held it like that, folded, her fingers trembling, for what could have been two minutes or twenty, already knowing what she'd find but somehow believing if she didn't open the letter, then the words couldn't hurt her. Finally, she pulled up her big-girl panties, unfolded the paper, smoothed it out on the counter and started to read.

She went through it a good four or five times before the message fully sank in. She let her purse slip through her fingers and fall to the floor with a dull *thunk*. A few seconds later, she slid down beside it and slumped against the cabinets, still clutching the note.

Ivy,
Andre called. The wedding's been moved up, and the bride needs an answer today. Call him. Take the job. I'll always treasure our time together, but I've got things to take care of at my place. Thanks for everything,
Cade.

She didn't need to say anything. He'd already decided everything for them, without so much as a by-your-leave.

She scrunched the offending paper into a ball and threw it across the room, as far away from her as her feeble pitching arm would carry it. Then she dug her cell back out of her purse and hit speed dial.

"Andre, it's Ivy," she said when he picked up, not bothering to let him say hello. She glared at the crumpled note, which had landed under the table. If she had heat vision, it would have burst into flames ten times over. "I've been thinking about that offer. I've never been to Belize. When would they need me there?"

"HARDESTY." O'BRIEN STUCK his damp head into the locker room. He'd clearly been working out, his SFD T-shirt stained with sweat and the veins in his arms still bulging with exertion. From the smug expression on his face, Cade knew it wasn't good news. "Captain wants to see you in his office."

"Be right there." He shoved his feet into his Vans, wiggled his toes and stood. Damn, it felt good being out of the cast and in regular footwear again. The one positive in his life since he'd run Ivy out of town three weeks ago.

"Better hurry," O'Brien taunted. "He looks pissed. You don't want to make him even madder by keeping him waiting."

His sweaty head disappeared.

"Thanks for the advice, ass-wipe," Cade mumbled to his retreating back. He slammed his locker shut and hoisted his duffel over his shoulder. His shift had been over hours ago, but he'd loitered at the station, helping stow the hoses and pack the gear, teaching the new probie how to make marinara sauce—Ivy's mom's recipe. Anything to avoid going home to his empty apartment.

He was beginning to wish he hadn't stuck around. As lonely as his nights had been since he'd moved out of the lake house, frozen dinners, cold beer and *American Ninja Warrior* beat the hell out of getting his ass chewed out by his boss.

He knocked on the office door and was rewarded with a curt "come in."

"You wanted to see me, Cappy?" Cade entered, closing the door behind him so all of C Company, currently on duty, wouldn't hear his butt-reaming. He stood at attention with his hands behind his back in front of Cappy's wide mahogany desk.

"Hardesty." Cappy's voice softened, and Cade relaxed a hair. Maybe this wasn't going to be as bad as O'Brien had led him to believe. "Sit down."

Cappy gestured to one of the two guest chairs. Cade sat and waited for his CO to steer the conversation.

"How's the leg?" Cappy asked.

"Good." Cade stretched his calf muscle reflexively. "Real good."

"I've got the doctor's report." Cappy tapped a manila file on the desk.

"And?" Cade leaned forward, elbows on his knees. He'd been back to work for a couple of weeks, but had only been cleared for light duty, so he was relegated to basic chores like cooking, cleaning and stocking shelves. Not exactly what he signed up for at the academy.

"You're good to go. Approved to return to active duty, no restrictions." Cade started to stand, but Cappy stopped him by holding up a hand, palm outward. "Physically. I'm concerned about your mental health."

"My mental health?"

"I heard through the grapevine you were living with that redhead from the softball game."

"In a manner of speaking." Cade leaned back, crossing an ankle over his knee. "What's that have to do with anything?"

"And that she left town a while ago."

"Something like that."

"Remember what you were like the last time you two hit a rough patch? Moody. Distracted. Going through the motions like a zombie. It puts everyone at risk. I can't have you like that again."

"I know, Cap. And you won't." Cade stood and offered his hand. "I promise."

"Your word is good enough for me." Cappy rose, took Cade's hand and shook it. "But I'll be keeping a close eye on you your first couple of weeks back."

"Understood." With a nod, Cade turned and headed for the door.

"Hardesty. One last thing."

Cade stopped, almost to the door, and spun back around to face his CO. "Yeah, Cap?"

"I hear you registered for the lieutenant exam." Cappy's eyes were hooded, his expression unreadable.

Cade nodded again, feeling like one of those bobblehead dolls they handed out every so often at Yankee Stadium. "I did."

"Good." Cappy gave what passed as a smile for him, and Cade let out a breath he didn't know he'd been holding. "You'd make a fine officer. If you need any help studying, let me know."

"Yes, sir."

Cade left the office feeling better than he had in weeks. Ivy was still gone, and nothing was going to change that. But at least now he had his job back, for real this time.

He whistled his way down the hall and out the engine bay, waving to his paramedic buddies in C Company as he went. He was just about to grab his keys out of his duffel when his cell rang. He pulled it out and swiped the screen without bothering to see who the call was from.

"Hey, butthead," Gabe greeted him. If you could call "butthead" a greeting. "Ready for me to kick your ass?"

Dammit.

"What took you so long?" Cade fumbled for his keys with his free hand and unlocked his SUV. This wasn't a discussion he wanted to have out in the parking lot.

"I was in Paris with Devin. She wanted to see the Louvre, and Noelle was performing there. But I'm here now. At the Half Pint, in fact. Waiting for you so I can kick your ass."

"You want me to voluntarily show up to my own ass

kicking?" Cade slid into the passenger seat and closed the door.

"The easier you make it for me, the easier I'll be on you."

"Fair enough." Cade put the key in the ignition and started the engine. "Be there in ten."

Why not? Gabe wasn't literally going to kick his ass, and there wasn't anything he could say that Cade hadn't already told himself.

He arrived eight minutes later. "He's over there." The blond who was behind the bar the last time he and Gabe had words at the Half Pint pointed Cade to a booth in the corner. "Said you wouldn't want an audience for the world of hurt he was going to lay on you."

Great. Maybe Gabe was planning on literally kicking his ass. Not that he didn't deserve it. He'd promised not to fuck with Ivy, yet that was exactly what he'd done, cutting her loose in the most chickenshit way possible. In a goddamn note.

Cade slipped into the booth opposite his soon-to-be-former best friend. Gabe pushed a mug of beer across the table to him. "Here. You're gonna need it."

"Thanks." Cade took a long, slow, fortifying drink.

"I saw Ivy in Paris," Gabe said, jumping right into the enormous, metaphorical pile of shit between them.

"How is she?" Cade asked.

"How do you think she is?" Gabe finished his beer and signaled the waitress for another. "Not that it's any of your business anymore."

"I still care about her."

"If you cared about her, you wouldn't have packed up all your stuff and moved out without a word."

What the hell? Was nothing secret in the Nelson family?

"I left a note," Cade said, sounding lame even to his own ears.

"Big man." Gabe paused to let the waitress set down his beer, nodding his thanks. "Three whole lines to kiss off the woman you sat in this bar and professed to love."

"I couldn't do it face-to-face." Cade stared into his beer.

"Then why do it at all?"

"Because she deserves better than this one-horse town. Better than me."

"That bullshit again?" Gabe reached across the table and smacked Cade on the back of the head. "You really are a moron."

"Ouch." Cade rubbed the nape of his neck. "That hurt."

"You're gonna hurt a lot more if you don't wise up."

"And do what? Drag her back here?"

"I don't think you'll need to resort to dragging," Gabe said. "She'll be here in a few days for that big calendar thing."

Crap. The Labor Day benefit. He'd forgotten about that. Even tossed the invitation when it had come in the mail. That stupid calendar had been the beginning of the end for him. The last place he wanted to be was a gala celebrating its release. He'd make a generous donation to salve his conscience and be done with it.

"I'm not going."

"Look, I probably shouldn't tell you this, but Ivy's a hot mess, thanks to you. Almost blew that big celebrity wedding."

Cade scratched his jaw. "That can't be true. I saw the pictures all over the internet. They looked fantastic."

"Her partner had to fly in last minute to pull her together."

"Andre?"

"That's him."

"Shit."

"Yeah."

The sat in silence for a few minutes, Gabe drinking his beer, Cade still staring into his. Gabe was the one to finally break it.

"She doesn't want that life anymore. Endless hotels and zero sleep. The models and the celebrity hissy fits. The stress. She's done with it."

"She says that now. But what about in…"

"Yeah, yeah, I know. Two years or three years or ten. But let me ask you this." Gabe pushed aside his mug and leaned in to pin his best courtroom stare on Cade. "You've known Ivy a long time. Have you ever known her to change her mind once she's decided on something?"

"No." He hadn't. He smiled, remembering Ivy at her most fearless, accepting every crazy dare they threw her way, never backing down, never giving up.

"Well, for some stupid-ass reason I don't even want to begin to understand, her mind's set on you." Gabe's prosecutor glare got even darker. "What are you going to do about that?"

"I'm not entirely sure." Cade chugged his beer, thumped the empty stein down on the table and stood. "But I'm going to start by digging my invitation to the calendar benefit out of the garbage."

"Good." Gabe sat back, the harsh lines around his eyes and mouth disappearing as his expression relaxed. "Because I haven't ruled out kicking your ass."

18

BELIZE WAS BEAUTIFUL, even in the rainy season. The deep, rich blue of the Caribbean, the bright colors and exotic sea life on the barrier reef, the easygoing charm of the beachside towns—Ivy loved it all.

She closed her eyes and breathed in the fresh salt air. Reclining in her beach chair, she stretched her arms over her head and dug her toes in the warm, fine sand.

It might be the rainy season, but in keeping with their charmed celebrity lives, the bride and groom had had sunshine for their nuptials, and the good weather stuck around for the remainder of the week. Lucky for Ivy, since the happy pair had offered her the run of the estate guesthouse for the remainder of their seven-day rental while they jetted off to honeymoon in an undisclosed location. It was more than she deserved, given her meltdown.

She took another long, deep breath, relishing the smells and sounds of the ocean—the rhythmic pounding of the waves against the shore and the calls of the seabirds flying overhead. The breeze ruffled the palm fronds, and she sighed. She was going to miss this place.

But she couldn't run forever. Sooner than she'd like—tomorrow morning, when her flight left Belize City—she'd have to face the music.

The music being the uncertain mess she'd made of her life.

"Are you sure you don't want me to come home with you, *ma mie*? You know how I love a good gala." Andre, her savior when she'd hit rock bottom, took up residence in the chair beside her and handed her another one of his fruity, alcoholic concoctions. She didn't ask, just drank. Whatever it was, it was bound to be delicious. Andre's creations always were.

"I appreciate the sentiment." She reached over and patted his arm with her free hand. "But you've done enough already, coming all the way here to rescue me. This is something I have to do myself."

Even if seeing Cade again would be the equivalent of ripping her heart out, stomping it to smithereens and putting it back in, just to rip it out and start the process all over again.

"Yes, it was a real hardship, traveling to an island paradise and snapping a few photographs." Andre gave her a bemused smile and sipped his own drink. "Not to mention waiting out the week here with nothing to do but imbibe, ingest and unwind."

"I'm sorry," Ivy said for what must have been the thousandth time. "I don't know what came over me. One minute I was scouting locations for the best backdrops, the next I was bawling like a baby."

Unfortunately for her, that minute was two days before the wedding. On the plus side, there had been enough time—barely—for Andre to hop a commercial flight, and the couple had agreed to the last-minute substitution.

"I'll tell you what came over you." He sat up, put his drink in a cup holder on the arm of his beach chair and took her hand between his. "*L'amour*. The thought of photographing a romantic destination wedding, with all the trimmings, was simply too much for you to bear with your recent *déchirement*."

"*Déchirement?*"

"Heartbreak."

"My heart is not broken." She sipped her drink. He'd mixed cranberry juice and grapefruit juice with some sort of alcohol. Rum, maybe. Or triple sec. She wasn't much of a drinker.

"*Menteuse.*" He gave her hand a quick squeeze before releasing it to reclaim his glass. "Liar."

Yeah, she was a big, fat liar, all right. If she was Pinocchio, her nose would be ten feet long.

Ivy lay back, closed her eyes and covered them with her forearm, hoping Andre would get the hint and end the conversation.

"Will your Prince Charming be at the ball?"

So much for subtlety. Picking up cues had never been Andre's strong suit. Or more likely he just chose to ignore them.

She sighed. "I assume so. He's one of the models."

"Aha!" Andre put his cup back in the holder and rubbed his hands together. "We must devise a plan."

"A plan?" She risked a glance at him from under her arm. "To do what?"

"Why, to win him back, *naturellement*."

"Who said anything about wanting to win him back?" Ivy abandoned the pretense of relaxing and sat up. "You forget, he dumped me. Via note. He didn't even have the courtesy to do it in person."

"Or the courage," Andre countered, sitting up beside her. "Have you considered that your Lothario might have thought he was doing what was best for you? And that writing a note was the only way he could do it without getting cold feet?"

"I don't understand." Ivy scrunched up her forehead. "In what possible world is getting dumped best for me?"

"If he hadn't broken up with you, would you have taken this job?"

"Probably not." She dragged a toe in the sand. "Definitely not."

"There you have it." Andre snapped his fingers decisively.

"But I didn't want this job." She wanted Cade. She cast an apologetic glance at Andre. "No offense."

"None taken." He nodded his acceptance of her apology. "But what if your young man…*comment s'appelle-t-il?*"

"Cade," she said.

"What if this Cade didn't want you sacrificing the career you worked so hard to build for him? So he made sure that wouldn't happen by ending things. A preemptive strike, if you will. A noble gesture."

"What sort of twisted logic is that?"

"Male logic." Andre chuckled.

"How do I combat that?"

"With feminine wiles."

"I don't think I remember what they are." Her chin trembled. "If I ever even had them."

"Fortunately for you, I'm an expert when it comes to wiles, male and female." With a flick of his wrist, Andre stood, bowed dramatically and held out his hand to her. "Come, *ma mie*. Let us scheme together."

She hesitated, biting her lip. "It sounds so…underhanded."

He dropped his hand. "Do you love him?"

This time she didn't have to think twice about her answer. "Yes. I've loved him forever."

"Do you think he loves you?"

Snapshots flicked through her brain. Cade, sweating in his turnouts for the sake of a few extra dollars for charity. Laughing as he patiently showed her how to play a game on his Xbox. Smiling down at her in the morning, his cornflower eyes dark with desire, touching her, tasting her, making her feel like she was the most beautiful woman in the world despite her morning breath and uncontrollable bedhead.

"I don't know." She nudged a stray hair behind her ear. "What if you're right, and he pushed me away because of some misguided sense of nobility?"

"There's only one way to find out."

"Feminine wiles?"

"Non." He shook his head. "I have changed my mind. For you, we must employ a simpler tactic."

"What's that?"

He held out his hand to her again. This time she took it and stood, wiggling her toes in the sand.

"You must seek him out at this calendar celebration. You must tell him how you feel. And you must ask him if he reciprocates those feelings."

Ivy suppressed a smile at Andre's formality. "You know you'll lose me if he says yes."

"C'est la vie." With a shrug, he put his arm around

her and steered her toward the palatial estate's guest house. "Life goes on."

"What will you do without me?" She rested her head on his shoulder as they walked.

"I shall weep. I shall mourn. I shall gnash my teeth and beat my breast." He kissed the top of her head. "And then I shall photograph your wedding, *bien sûr*."

"MY DEAR." MRS. THORPE, president of the local chapter of the Humane Society and chairwoman of the shelter benefit, hurried over to Ivy the minute she stepped into the gym at Stockton High School. "We're so glad you could join us. The calendar turned out beautifully."

"I wouldn't miss it, Mrs. Thorpe. And thank you." Ivy smiled and kissed the older woman's cheek, admiring her classic Diane von Furstenberg sheath dress and matching pumps. It was nice to see a familiar face straight off. Hopefully a sign things would go smoothly and the evening would turn out the way she wanted. "You look lovely tonight. How's Paco?"

"He's fine, the little scamp. Loves the rubber stick you gave him. So much safer than the real ones. No nasty splinters." She shuddered at the thought of her precious Chihuahua injured by a rogue piece of wood. "And if I've told you once I've told you a thousand times, dear, call me Susan."

"I'm sorry. Susan."

"Come on." The older woman hooked her arm through Ivy's. "I've reserved a seat for you in the front row, next to me. The runway show is starting soon."

"Runway show?"

For the first time since she entered the gym, Ivy took note of her surroundings. The event committee had done a bang-up job transforming it into something befitting New York Fashion Week. At one end—where Mrs. Thorpe was dragging her to now—they'd set up a platform in the shape of a *T*, backed by dark curtains that ran the length of the far wall. Along the leg of the *T* were rows of chairs, which were quickly filling with spectators. Half the town must be there, Ivy thought. She caught sight of her parents on the other side of the stage and waved.

"We're featuring some of our calendar models, each with a pet that's up for adoption," Mrs. Thorpe explained as they made their way across the darkened gym to the stage. The usual harsh, fluorescent lights had been by-passed in favor of strobes and a disco ball. LEDs lined the edges of the runway. "We're hoping to make some matches."

"For the models or the pets?" Ivy quipped, her palms starting to sweat as she thought about one particular blond, blue-eyed model.

"The pets, but I saw a few of the models getting ready backstage and I wouldn't be surprised if they got more than their fair share of offers, too." Mrs. Thorpe gave Ivy a saucy wink and directed her to two empty seats.

"Do you happen to know if Cade Hardesty is model-ing this evening?" Ivy asked hesitantly as she sat down, crossing her legs and smoothing out the skirt of her dress—a black-and-white checked Betsey Johnson pinup number Andre had insisted she buy. If Cade was walk-ing the runway, she'd be close enough to touch him. And although she'd planned on seeing him tonight, somehow she'd imagined their first encounter being a bit more... private.

"Which one is he?" Mrs. Thorpe asked a little too

innocently. "They're all so handsome. Like my Roger in his day."

"Mr. December," Ivy answered, figuring that was the quickest way to identify him.

"Oh, him." Oh. My. God. Had Mrs. Thorpe actually licked her lips? "He's our final attraction. The main event."

The main event?

Ivy fingered her pearl choker, the perfect accessory for her fifties-inspired, cleavage-enhancing dress. "What does that—"

"Shh." Mrs. Thorpe held a finger to her lips as the volume of the music increased and the mayor stepped out from the curtains onto the stage. "It's starting."

The mayor, who was acting as emcee for the evening, introduced each model and their canine or feline companion. Mr. January started things off with a bang in just his bunker pants, suspenders dangling from his waist, carrying a yippy Pomeranian called Lulu. Mr. April wore a tight SFD tank top with his turnouts and was accompanied by the ugliest cat Ivy had ever seen, a hairless thing the mayor said was hypoallergenic and appropriately named Kojak. As the pairs strutted their respective stuff, the pets were auctioned off to eager buyers for adoption.

"Sold to the Levensons for five hundred dollars." The mayor nodded to Mr. November as he left the stage with his companion, an adorable German shepherd puppy that had commandeered the highest price of the night so far. Ivy recognized the model as one of Cade's friends. Hansen, she thought. Or Sykes. She kept mixing them up. She probably should have paid better attention when the mayor was introducing him, but with Cade up next her brain was running a million miles a minute.

"Thank you, Mr. November and Axel," the mayor continued. "I'm sure you'll be very happy in your new home. Axel, that is. Not Mr. November."

The audience chuckled at the mayor's joke, and she acknowledged them with a mock bow. "Remember, all our models will be signing calendars after the show tonight. They're only twenty-five dollars each, and they make a great gift. The calendars, that is. Not the models."

The audience laughed again, and the mayor grinned. "And now for our final pair of the evening. I give you Mr. December and Piper."

Ivy held her breath. The curtains parted and Cade appeared. A collective gasp echoed through the crowd as he strutted down the runway almost naked, in the Santa hat and G-string he'd worn at the photo shoot. He held a tabby kitten, which snuggled against his broad chest.

"Now that's what I call a Christmas present," Mrs. Thorpe observed with an appreciative whistle.

"You can say that again," Ivy muttered.

"What's that, dear?" Mrs. Thorpe asked.

"Never mind." Ivy ducked her head, a hot flush creeping up her cheeks.

"Well, don't look now," Mrs. Thorpe said, nudging her, "but he's coming your way."

Ivy's head jerked up. Mrs. Thorpe was right. Cade was headed straight for her, his impossibly blue eyes shining with determination.

Shit, shit, shit, shit, shit, shit, shit. This was not how their big reunion was supposed to happen. She had it all planned out. She was going to get him alone, in some secluded corner, and then she'd...

"Hey, Ivy," he said over the music playing in the background.

His voice was a sexy rumble that sent her pulse pounding. He crouched down on the runway so that those damned baby blues were almost on her eye level.

"Hey," she croaked. An inauspicious beginning.

"This is Piper, and he's got something to ask you."

He held the kitten out to her. She took it, rubbing between its ears. "Piper?"

The crowd had started to stir, a discontented murmur rolling through it like thunder before a storm. Even the mayor, standing helplessly behind Cade on the runway, looked confused. Only Mrs. Thorpe, sitting calmly next to her, appeared suspiciously unconcerned about the strange turn of events.

"He's the little guy we rescued from the drainpipe."

"Oh." Ivy buried her nose in the cat's soft fur. "Does he need a home?"

"No." Cade swallowed, his Adam's apple bobbing in his throat. "We do."

"We?"

He jumped off the stage and kneeled down in front of her. Everything else—the music, the mayor, Mrs. Thorpe, the crowd—faded as he put the kitten in her lap and took her hands in his.

"I screwed up. I'm a guy, and I'm stupid and I screwed up. And I'll probably screw up again."

"Not the best advertisement for yourself," Mrs. Thorpe chimed in. "Get to the good stuff."

"Right." He gave the older woman an appreciative smile then turned his attention back to Ivy. "The good stuff. The good stuff is that I'm in love with you. And I'm pretty sure, I mean, I think… I mean, I hope you're in love with me, too."

"Now you're warming up." Mrs. Thorpe reached over and plucked the squirming kitten out of Ivy's lap before it could wriggle onto the floor. "Close the deal."

"Marry me, Ivy."

"What?" she squeaked.

Mrs. Thorpe slipped him a small, velvet box, which he flicked open to reveal a stunning, pear-shaped diamond. "Marry me."

She opened her mouth, but no words came out.

"I pushed you away because I thought it was the right thing to do. I didn't want to hold you back. But I was wrong. Very wrong. I don't care if you spend half your life flying across the globe taking fabulous photographs, as long as you spend the other half here, with me."

He looked up at her, those clear blue eyes pleading. "You're my home, Ivy. Let me be yours."

"Answer him, honey, or I will," Mrs. Thorpe teased.

"Come on, Ivy." Cade took the ring out of the box and dangled it in front of her. "I dare you. And you know you can't resist a dare."

"It's you I can't resist, you big dope." She held out her left hand, shaking.

"Is that a yes?"

"Yes, it's a yes. To you and Piper."

"Thank God." He slipped the ring on her finger, pulled her to her feet and kissed her. It was a kiss that was different from the others they'd shared, as simultaneously thrilling and tender as before but with something more. A knowledge that, from this day forward, all his kisses were hers, as hers were his. He deepened the kiss and she followed, throwing her arms around his neck and losing herself in the gentle pressure of his lips.

"She said yes," Mrs. Thorpe announced, standing and holding the cat up like Simba in *The Lion King*.

The crowd burst into applause and Ivy, suddenly aware that almost the entire town was watching them, broke off the kiss and buried her face against his chest. "I can't believe you did this in front of everyone. In a G-string. Oh, my God, my parents—"

"Were in on the whole thing. As was Mrs. Thorpe. It's hard to hide a ring in a G-string." With one arm around Ivy, he used the other to take the older woman's wrinkled hand, bring it to his lips and kiss it. "You were a perfect accomplice."

"Anytime. I haven't had so much fun since my Roger and I went to Vegas for our second honeymoon. We won a thousand dollars playing blackjack and spent it all on tickets to see Celine Dion." She handed the kitten to Ivy. "Now, quick. You two run along. And put some clothes on, young man. You're engaged now. Can't be flaunting the goods and making all the rest of us gals jealous."

"Yes, ma'am." Cade hoisted Ivy up into his arms, cradling her against his chest. Piper mewled in protest.

"What are you doing?" she shrieked, attracting even more applause as they made their way through the crowd.

"Following orders."

"I don't recall Mrs. Thorpe ordering you to pick me up and carry me off."

"It's all in the interpretation." He found a gap in the curtain at the back of the runway and ducked behind it. "And don't pretend you haven't always wanted to play fireman with me."

"You've got me there," she admitted, admiring the play of the muscles in his chest and arms.

He carried her all the way to one of the classrooms. From the look of it—clothes strewn everywhere—the models had been using it as a dressing room. He set her down and locked the door.

"What about the others?"

"They're busy signing calendars."

"Shouldn't you be, too?"

"This is more important." He took Piper from her and set the kitten down on the floor. "I meant what I said. You don't have to give up your career. I can travel with you when I'm free. One of the guys at the station will take care of Piper. And when I'm not—"

"Wait." She put a finger to his lips for a moment. "I have something to tell you. You know where the bookstore used to be?"

"Sure. On Main Street, two doors down from Maude's."

"I signed a one-year lease this morning."

"A lease?"

"For my studio. Hank's retiring. Seems he enjoyed his time off a little too much. He's turning over his customers to me. The place is going to need a lot of work, but—"

This time it was Cade who silenced her, and not with his finger but with his lips.

"Are you sure?" he asked when they came up for air. "This is really what you want?"

She reached up to brush a lock of hair off his forehead. "You're what I want."

"And you're what I want." He kissed her again, slow and sensuous, until the kitten mewed at their feet and they broke apart, laughing.

"I guess we better get the little guy home," she said, bending down for a moment to scratch Piper between the ears.

"No can do. Like you pointed out, I've got calendars to sign."

"Tell you what. Go out there and do your thing, and Piper and I will be at your place waiting for you."

"Not my place," he corrected. "Our place. Home."

"Home." She kissed his jaw. "My new favorite word in the English language."

He gathered her close, his strong arms circling her waist. "Mine, too."

* * * * *

*If you like fun, sexy and steamy stories with strong
heroines and irresistible heroes, you'll love
THE HARDER YOU FALL by* New York Times
bestselling author Gena Showalter—*featuring
Jessie Kay Dillon and Lincoln West, the sexy bachelor
who's breaking all his rules for this
rowdy Southern belle...*

*Turn the page for a sneak peek at
THE HARDER YOU FALL!*

WEST HAD BROUGHT a date.

The realization hit Jessie Kay like a bolt of lightning in a freak storm. Great! Wonderful! While she'd opted not to bring Daniel, and thus make West the only single person present—and embarrassingly alone—he'd chosen his next two-month "relationship" and hung Jessie Kay out to dry.

Hidden in the back of the sanctuary, Jessie Kay stood in the doorway used by church personnel and scowled. Harlow had asked for—cough, banshee-screeched, cough—a status report. Jessie Kay had abandoned her precious curling iron in order to sneak a peek at the guys.

Now she pulled her phone out of the pocket in her dress to text Daniel. Oops. She'd missed a text.

Sunny: Party 2nite?????

She made a mental note to respond to Sunny later and drafted her note to Daniel.

I'm at the church. How fast can you get here? I need a friend/date for Harlow's wedding

A response didn't come right away. She knew he'd gone on a date last night and the girl had stayed the night with him. How did she know? Because he'd texted Jessie Kay to ask how early he could give the snoring girl the boot.

Sooo glad I never hooked up with him.

Finally, a vibration signaled a response.

Any other time I'd race to your rescue, even though weddings are snorefests. Today I'm in the city on a job

He'd started some kind of high-risk security firm with a few of his Army buddies.

Her: Fine. You suck. I clearly need to rethink our friendship

Daniel: I'll make it up to you, swear. Want to have dinner later???

She slid her phone back in place without responding, adding his name to her mental note. If he wasn't going to ignore his responsibilities whenever she had a minor need, he deserved to suffer for a little while.

Of its own accord, Jessie Kay's gaze returned to West. The past week, she'd seen him only twice. Both times, she'd gone to the farmhouse to help her sister with sandwiches and casseroles, and he'd taken one look at her, grabbed his keys and driven off.

Would it have killed him to acknowledge her presence by calling her by some hateful name, per usual? After all, he'd had the nerve to flirt with her at the diner, to look at her as if she'd stripped naked and begged him to have *her* for dessert. And now he ignored her? Men! This one in particular.

Her irritation grew as he introduced his date to Kenna Starr and her fiancé, Dane Michaelson. Kenna was a stunning redhead who'd always been Brook Lynn's partner in crime. The girl who'd done what Jessie Kay had not, saving her sister every time she'd gotten into trouble.

Next up was an introduction to Daphne Roberts, the mother of Jase's nine-year-old daughter, Hope, then Brad Lintz, Daphne's boyfriend.

Jase and Beck joined the happy group, but the brunette never looked away from West, as if he was speaking the good Lord's gospel. Her adoration was palpable.

A sharp pang had Jessie Kay clutching her chest. *Too young for a heart attack.*

Indigestion?

Yeah. Had to be.

The couple should have looked odd together. West was too tall and the brunette was far too short for him. A skyscraper next to a one-story house. But somehow, despite their height difference, the two actually complemented each other.

And really, the girl's adoration had to be good for West, buoying him the way Daniel's praise often buoyed Jessie Kay. Only on a much higher level, considering the girl was more than a friend to West.

Deep down, Jessie Kay was actually…happy for West. As crappy as his childhood had been, he deserved a nice slice of contentment.

Look at me, acting like a big girl and crap.

When West wrapped his arm around the brunette's waist, drawing her closer, Jessie Kay's nails dug into her palms.

I'm happy for him, remember? Besides, big girls didn't want to push other women in front of a speeding bus.

Jessie Kay's phone buzzed. Another text. This one from Brook Lynn.

Hurry! Bridezilla is on a rampage!!!

Her: Tell her the guys look amazing in their tuxes—no stains or tears yet—and the room is gorgeous. Or just tell her NOTHING HAS FREAKING CHANGED

The foster bros had gone all out even though the ceremony was to be a small and intimate affair. There were red and white roses at the corner of every pew, and in front of the pulpit was an ivory arch with wispy jewel-encrusted lace.

With a sigh, she added an adorable smiley face to her message, because it was cute and it said I'm not yelling at you. My temper is not engaged.

Send.

Brook Lynn: Harlow wants a play-by-play of the action

Fine.

Beck is now speaking w/Pastor Washington. Jase, Dane, Kenna, Daphne & Brad are engaged in conversation, while Hope is playing w/ her doll on the floor. Happy?

She didn't add that West was focused on the stunning brunette, who was still clinging to his side.

The girl…she had a familiar face—*where have I seen her?*—and a body so finely honed Jessie Kay wanted to stuff a few thousand Twinkies down her throat just to make it fair for the rest of the female population. Her designer dress was made of ebony silk and hugged her curves like a besotted lover.

Like West would be doing tonight?

Grinding her teeth, Jessie Kay slid her gaze over her own gown. One she'd sewn in her spare time. Not bad— actually kind of awesome—but compared to Great Bod's delicious apple it was a rotten orange.

A wave of jealousy swept over her. Dang it! Jealousy was stupid. Jessie Kay was no can of dog food in the looks department. In fact, she was well able to hold her own against anyone, anywhere, anytime. But…but…

A lot of baggage came with her.

West suddenly stiffened, as if he knew he was being watched. He turned. Her heart slamming against her ribs with enough force to break free and escape, she darted into Harlow's bridal chamber—the choir room.

Harlow finished curling her thick mass of hair as Brook Lynn gave her lips a final swipe of gloss.

"Welcome to my nightmare," Jessie Kay announced. "I might as well put in rollers, pull on a pair of mom jeans and buy ten thousand cats." Cats! Want! "I'm officially an old maid without any decent prospects."

Brook Lynn wrinkled her brow. "What are you talking about?"

"Everyone is here, including West and his date. I'm the only single person in our group, which means you guys have to set me up with your favorite guy friends. Obviously I'm looking for a nine or ten. Make it happen. Please and thank you."

Harlow went still. "West brought a date? Who is it?"

Had a curl of steam just risen from her nostrils? "Just some girl."

Harlow pressed her hands against a stomach that had to be dancing with nerves. "I don't want *just some girl* at my first wedding."

"You planning your divorce to Beck already?"

Harlow scowled at her. "Not funny. You know we're planning a larger ceremony next year."

Jessie Kay raised her hands, palms out. "You're right, you're right. And you totally convinced me. I'll kick the bitch out pronto." *And I'll love every second of it—on Harlow's behalf.*

"No. No. I don't want a scene." Stomping her foot, Harlow added, "What was West thinking? He's ruined *everything.*"

Ooo-kay. A wee bit dramatic, maybe. "I doubt he was thinking at all. If that boy ever had an idea, it surely died of loneliness." Too much? "Anyway. I'm sure you could use a glass or six of champagne. I'll open the bottle for us—for you. You're welcome."

A wrist corsage hit her square in the chest.

"This is *my* day, Jessica Dillon." Harlow thumped her chest. "Mine! You will remain stone-cold sober, or I will remove your head, place it on a stick and wave it around while your sister sobs over your bleeding corpse."

Wow. "That's pretty specific, but I feel you. No alcohol for me, ma'am." She gave a jaunty salute. "I mean, no alcohol for me, Miss Bridezilla, sir."

"Ha-ha." Harlow morphed from fire-breathing dragon to fairy-tale princess in an instant, twirling in a circle. "Now stop messing around and tell me how amazing I look. And don't hesitate to use words like *exquisite* and *magical.*"

The hair at her temples had been pulled back, but the

rest hung to her elbows in waves so dark they glimmered blue in the light. The gown had capped sleeves and a straight bustline with a cinched-in waist and pleats that flowed all the way to the floor, covering the sensible flats she'd chosen based on West's advice. "You look... exquisitely magical."

"Magically exquisite," Brook Lynn said with a nod.

"My scars aren't hideous?" Self-conscious, Harlow smoothed a hand over the multitude of jagged pink lines running between her breasts, courtesy of an attack she'd miraculously survived as a teenage girl.

"Are you kidding? Those scars make you look bad-ass." Jessie Kay curled a few more pieces of hair, adding, "I'm bummed my skin is so flawless."

Harlow snorted. "Yes, let's shed a tear for you."

Jessie Kay gave her sister the stink eye. "You better not be like this for your wedding. I won't survive two of you."

Brook Lynn held up her well-manicured hands, all innocence.

"Well." She glanced at a wristwatch she wasn't wearing, doing her best impression of West. "We've got twenty minutes before the festivities kick off. Need anything?"

Harlow's hands returned to her stomach, the color draining from her cheeks in a hurry. "Yes. Beck."

Blinking, certain she'd misheard, she fired off a quick "Excuse me?" Heck. Deck. Neck. Certainly not Beck. "Grooms aren't supposed to see—"

"I need Beck." Harlow stomped her foot. *"Now."*

"Have you changed your mind?" Brook Lynn asked. "If so, we'll—"

"No, no. Nothing like that." Harlow launched into a quick pace, marching back and forth through the room.

"I just… I need to see him. He hates change, and this is the biggest one of all, and I need to talk to him before I totally. Flip. Out. Okay? All right?"

"This isn't that big a change, honey. Not really." Who would have guessed Jessie Kay would be a voice of reason in a situation like this. Or *any* situation? "You guys live together already."

"Beck!" she insisted. "Beck, Beck, Beck."

"Temper tantrums are not attractive." Jessie Kay shared a concerned look with her sister, who nodded. "All right. One Beck coming up." As fast as her heels would allow, she made her way back to the sanctuary.

She purposely avoided West's general direction, focusing only on the groom. "Harlow has decided to throw millions of years' worth of tradition out the window. She wants to see you without delay. Are you wearing a cup? I'd wear a cup. Good luck."

He'd been in the middle of a conversation with Jase, and like Harlow, he quickly paled. "Is something wrong with her?" He didn't stick around for an answer, rushing past Jessie Kay without actually judging the distance between them, almost knocking her over.

As she stumbled, West flew over and latched on to her wrist to help steady her. The contact nearly buckled her knees. His hands were calloused, his fingers firm. His strength unparalleled and his skin hot enough to burn. Electric tingles rushed through her, the world around her fading from existence until they were the only two people in existence.

Fighting for every breath, she stared up at him. His gaze dropped to her lips and narrowed, his focus savagely carnal and primal in its possessiveness, as if he saw nothing else, either—wanted nothing and no one else ever. But as he slowly lowered his arm and stepped away from her, the world snapped back into motion.

The bastard brought a date.

Right. She cleared her throat, embarrassed by the force of her reaction to him. "Thanks."

A muscle jumped in his jaw. A sign of anger? "May I speak with you privately?"

Uh… "Why?"

"Please."

What the what now? Had Lincoln West actually said the word *please* to her? *Her?* "Whatever you have to say to me—" an insult, no doubt "—can wait. You should return to your flavor of the year." Opting for honesty, she grudgingly added, "You guys look good together."

The muscle jumped again, harder, faster. "You think we look good together?"

"Very much so." Two perfect people. "I'm not being sarcastic, if that's what you're getting at. Who is she?"

"Monica Gentry. Fitness guru based in the city."

Well. That explained the sense of familiarity. And the body. Jessie Kay had once briefly considered thinking about exercising along with Monica's video. Then she'd found a bag of KIT KAT Minis and the insane idea went back to hell, where it belonged. "She's a good choice for you. Beautiful. Successful. Driven. And despite what you think about me, despite the animosity between us, I want you happy."

And not just because of his crappy childhood, she realized. He was a part of her family, for better or worse. A girl made exceptions for family. Even the douche bags.

His eyes narrowed to tiny slits. "We're going to speak

privately, Jessie Kay, whether you agree or not. The only decision you need to make is whether or not you'll walk. I'm more than willing to carry you."

A girl also had the right to smack family. "You're just going to tell me to change my hideous dress, and I'm going to tell you I'm fixing to cancel your birth certificate."

When Harlow had proclaimed *Wear whatever you want*, Jessie Kay had done just that, creating a bloodred, off-the-shoulder, pencil-skirt dress that molded to her curves like a second skin...made from leftover material for drapes.

Scarlett O'Hara has nothing on me!

Jessie Kay was proud of her work, but she wasn't blind to its flaws. Knotted threads in the seams. Years had passed since she'd sewn anything, and her skills were rusty.

West gave her another once—twice—over as fire smoldered in his eyes. "Why would I tell you to change?" His voice dipped, nothing but smoke and gravel. "You and that dress are a fantasy come true."

Uh, what the what now? Had Lincoln West just called her *a fantasy*?

Almost can't process...

"Maybe you should take me to the ER, West. I think I just had a brain aneurysm." She rubbed her temples. "I'm hallucinating."

"Such a funny girl." He ran his tongue over his teeth, snatched her hand and while Monica called his name, dragged Jessie Kay to a small room in back. A cleaning closet, the air sharp with antiseptic. What little space was available was consumed by overstuffed shelves.

"When did you decide to switch careers and become a caveman?" she asked.

"When you decided to switch careers and become a femme fatale."

Have mercy on my soul.

He released her to run his fingers through his hair, leaving the strands in sexy spikes around his head. "Listen. I owe you an apology for the way I've treated you in the past. The way I've acted today. I shouldn't have manhandled you, and I'm very sorry."

Her eyes widened. Seriously, what the heck had happened to this man? In five minutes, he'd upended everything she'd come to expect from him.

And he wasn't done! "I'm sorry for every hurtful thing I've ever said to you. I'm sorry for making you feel bad about who you are and what you've done. I'm sorry—"

"Stop. Just stop." She placed her hands over her ears in case he failed to heed her order. "I don't understand what's happening."

He gently removed her hands and held on tight to her wrists. "What's happening? I'm owning my mistakes and hoping you're in a forgiving mood."

"You want to be my friend?" The words squeaked from her.

"I...do."

Why the hesitation? "Here's the problem. You're a dog and I'm a cat, and we're never going to get along."

One corner of his mouth quirked with lazy amusement, causing a flutter to skitter through her pulse. "I think you're wrong...kitten."

Kitten. A freakishly adorable nickname, and absolutely perfect for her. But also absolutely unexpected.

Oh, she'd known he'd give her one sooner or later. He and his friends enjoyed renaming the women in their lives. Jase always called Brook Lynn "angel" and Beck called Harlow everything from "beauty" to "hag," her initials. Well, HAG prewedding. But Jessie Kay had prepared herself for "demoness" or the always classic "bitch."

"Dogs and cats can be friends," he said, "especially when the dog minds his manners. I promise you, things will be different from now on."

"Well." Reeling, she could come up with no witty reply. "We could try, I guess."

"Good." His gaze dropped to her lips, heated a few more degrees. "Now all we have to do is decide what kind of friends we should be."

Her heart started kicking up a fuss all over again, breath abandoning her lungs. "What do you mean?"

"Text frequently? Call each other occasionally? Only speak when we're with our other friends?" He backed her into a shelf and cans rattled, threatening to fall. "Or should we be friends with benefits?"

The tingles returned, sweeping over her skin and sinking deep, deep into bone. Her entire body ached with sudden need and it was so powerful it nearly felled her. How long since a man had focused the full scope of his masculinity on her? Too long and never like this. Somehow West had reduced her to a quivering mess of femininity and whoremones.

"I vote…we only speak when we're with our other friends," she said, embarrassed by the breathless tremor in her voice.

"What if I want all of it?" He placed his hands at her

temples and several of the cans rolled to the floor. "The texts, the calls…and the benefits."

"No?" A question? Really? "No to the last. You have a date."

He scowled at her as if *she'd* done something wrong. "See, that's the real problem, kitten. I don't want her. I want you."

WEST CALLED HIMSELF a thousand kinds of fool. He'd planned to apologize, return to the sanctuary, witness his friend's wedding and start the countdown with Monica. The moment he'd gotten Jessie Kay inside the closet, her pecans-and-cinnamon scent in his nose, those plans burned to ash. Only one thing mattered.

Getting his hands on her.

From day one, she'd been a vertical g-force too strong to deny, pulling, pulling, *pulling* him into a bottomless vortex. He'd fought it every minute of every day since meeting her, and he'd gotten nowhere fast. Why not give in? Stop the madness?

Just once…

"We've been dancing around this for months," he said. "I'm scum for picking here and now to hash this out with you, and I'll care tomorrow. Right now, I think it's time we did something about our feelings."

"I don't…" She began to soften against him, only to snap to attention. "No. Absolutely not. I can't."

"You *won't.*" *But I can change your mind…*

She nibbled on her bottom lip.

Something he would kill to do. So he did it. He leaned into her, caught her bottom lip between his teeth and ran the plump morsel through. "Do you want me, Jessie Kay?"

Her eyes closed for a moment, a shiver rocking her. "You say you'll care tomorrow, so I'll give you an answer then. As for today, I... I... I'm leaving." But she made no effort to move away, and he knew. She did want him. As badly as he wanted her. "Yes. Leaving. Any moment now..."

Acting without thought—purely on instinct—he placed his hands on her waist and pressed her against the hard line of his body. "I want you to stay. I want you, period."

"West." The new tremor in her voice injected his every masculine instinct with adrenaline, jacking him up. "You said it yourself. You're scum. This is wrong."

Anticipation raced denial to the tip of his tongue, and won by a photo finish. "Do you care?" He caressed his way to her ass and cupped the perfect globes, then urged her forward to rub her against the long length of his erection. The woman who'd tormented his days and invaded his dreams moaned a decadent sound of satisfaction and it did something to him. Made his need for her *worse.*

She wasn't what he should want, but somehow she'd become everything he could not resist, and he was tired, so damn tired, of walking, hell, running away from her.

"Do you?" he insisted. "Say yes, and *I'll* be the one to leave. I don't want you to regret this." He wanted her desperate for more.

She looked away from him, licked her lips. "Right at this moment? No. I don't care." As soft as a whisper.

Triumph filled him, his clasp on her tightening.

"But tomorrow..." she added.

Yes. Tomorrow. He wasn't the only one who'd been running from the sizzle between them, but today, with her admission ringing in his ears, he wasn't letting her get away. One look at her, that's all it had taken to ruin his plans. Now she would pay the price. Now she would make everything better.

"I *will* regret it," she said. "This is a mistake I've made too many times in the past."

Different emotions played over her features. Features so delicate he was consumed by the need to protect her from anything and anyone…but himself.

He saw misery, desire, fear, regret, hope and anger. The anger concerned him. This Southern belle could knock a man's testicles into his throat with a single swipe of her knee. Even still, West didn't walk away.

"For all we know, the world will end tomorrow. Let's focus on today. You tell me what you want me to do," he said, nuzzling his nose against her cheek, "and I'll do it."

More tremors rocked her. She traced her delicate hands up his tie and gave the knot a little shake, an action that was sexy, sweet and wicked all at once. "I want you…to go back to your date. You and I, we'll be friends as agreed, and we'll pretend this never happened." She pushed him, but he didn't budge.

His date. Yeah, he'd forgotten about Monica before Jessie Kay had mentioned her a few minutes ago. But then, he'd gotten used to forgetting everything whenever the luscious blonde entered a room. Everything about her consumed every part of him, and it was more than irritating, it was a sickness to be cured, an obstacle to be overcome and an addiction to be avoided. If they did this, he would suffer from his own regrets, but there was no question he would love the ride.

He bunched up the hem of her skirt, his fingers brushing the silken heat of her bare thigh. Her breath hitched, driving him wild. "You've told me what you *think* you should want me to do." He rasped the words against her mouth, hovering over her, not touching her but teasing with what could be. "Now tell me what you really want me to do."

Navy blues peered up at him, beseeching; the fight drained out of her, leaving only need and raw vulnerability. "I'm only using you for sex—said no guy ever. But that's what you're going to do. Isn't it? You're going to use me and lose me, just like the others."

Her features were utterly *ravaged*, and in that moment, he hated himself. Because she was right. Whether he took her for a single night or every night for two months, the end result would be the same. No matter how much it hurt her—no matter how much it hurt *him*—he would walk away.

COMING NEXT MONTH FROM

HARLEQUIN *Blaze*

Available December 15, 2015

#875 PLEASING HER SEAL
Uniformly Hot!
by Anne Marsh
Wedding blogger Madeline Holmes lives and breathes romance—from the sidelines. That is, until Navy SEAL Mason Black promises to fulfill all of her fantasies at an exclusive island resort. But is Mason her ultimate fantasy—could he be "the one"?

#876 RED HOT
Hotshot Heroes
by Lisa Childs
Forest ranger firefighter Wyatt Andrews battles the flames to keep others safe, but who will protect *him* from the fiery redhead who thinks he's endangering her little brother?

#877 HER SEXY VEGAS COWBOY
by Ali Olson
Jessica Gainey decides to take a wild ride with rancher Aaron Weathers while she's in Vegas. But when it's time to go home, how can she put those hot nights—and her sexy cowboy—behind her?

#878 PLAYING TO WIN
by Taryn Leigh Taylor
Reporter Holly Evans is determined to uncover star hockey captain Luke Maguire's sinful secrets. But when *he's* the one who turns the heat up on *her*, their sexy game is on...

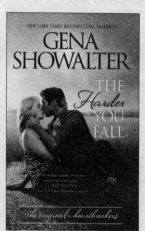

SPECIAL EXCERPT FROM

HARLEQUIN *Blaze*

*When Maddie Holmes first meets Mason Black she has
no idea he's a Navy SEAL on an undercover mission...
but she's about to find out all his secrets!*

Read on for a sneak preview of
PLEASING HER SEAL by **Anne Marsh**
part of Harlequin Blaze's
UNIFORMLY HOT! *miniseries.*

Fantasy Island advertised itself as an idyllic slice of
paradise located on the Caribbean Sea—the perfect place
for a destination wedding or honeymoon. The elegant type
on the resort brochure promised barefoot luxury, discreet
hedonism and complete wish fulfillment. Maddie's job
was to translate those naughty promises into sexy web
copy that would drive traffic to her blog and fill her bank
account with much-needed advertising dollars.

The summit beckoned, and she stepped out into a
small clearing overlooking the ocean.

"Good view?" At the sound of the deep male voice
behind her, Maddie flinched, arms and legs jerking
in shock. Her camera flew forward as she scrambled
backward.

Strong male fingers fastened around her wrist. Panicked, she grabbed her croissant and lobbed it at the guy,
followed by her coffee. He cursed and dodged.

"It's not a good day to jump without a chute." He
tugged her away from the edge of the lookout, and she
got her first good look at him. Not a stranger. *Okay, then.*

HBEXP1215

Her heart banged hard against her rib cage, pummeling her lungs, before settling back into a more normal rhythm. *Mason.* Mason I-Can't-Be-Bothered-To-Tell-You-My-Last-Name-But-I'm-A-Stud. He led the cooking classes by the pool. She'd written him off as good-looking but aloof, not certain if she'd spotted a spark of potential interest in his dark eyes. Wishful thinking or dating potential—it was probably a moot point now, since she'd just pegged him with her mocha.

He didn't seem pissed off. On the contrary, he simply rocked back on his haunches, hands held out in front of him. *I come in peace*, she thought, fortunately too out of breath to giggle. The side of his shirt sported a dark stain from her coffee. Oh, goody. She'd actually scalded him. Way to make an impression on a poor, innocent guy. This was why her dating life sucked.

She tried to wheeze out an apology, but he shook his head.

"I scared you."

"You think?"

"That wasn't my intention." The look on his face was part chagrin, part repentance. Worked for her.

"I'll put a bell around your neck." Where had he learned to move so quietly?

"Why don't we start over?" He stuck out a hand. A big, masculine, slightly muddy hand. She probably shouldn't want to seize his fingers like a lifeline. "I'm Mason Black."

Don't miss PLEASING HER SEAL by Anne Marsh, available January 2016 wherever Harlequin® Blaze® books and ebooks are sold.

www.Harlequin.com

HBEXP1215

REQUEST YOUR FREE BOOKS!
2 FREE NOVELS PLUS 2 FREE GIFTS!

HARLEQUIN®

Blaze®

red-hot reads!

YES! Please send me 2 FREE Harlequin® Blaze® novels and my 2 FREE gifts (gifts are worth about $10). After receiving them, if I don't wish to receive any more books, I can return the shipping statement marked "cancel." If I don't cancel, I will receive 4 brand-new novels every month and be billed just $4.74 per book in the U.S. or $5.21 per book in Canada. That's a savings of at least 14% off the cover price. It's quite a bargain. Shipping and handling is just 50¢ per book in the U.S. and 75¢ per book in Canada.* I understand that accepting the 2 free books and gifts places me under no obligation to buy anything. I can always return a shipment and cancel at any time. Even if I never buy another book, the two free books and gifts are mine to keep forever.

150/350 HDN GH2D

Name _____ (PLEASE PRINT)

Address _____ Apt. #

City _____ State/Prov. _____ Zip/Postal Code

Signature (if under 18, a parent or guardian must sign)

Mail to the **Reader Service:**
IN U.S.A.: P.O. Box 1867, Buffalo, NY 14240-1867
IN CANADA: P.O. Box 609, Fort Erie, Ontario L2A 5X3

Want to try two free books from another line?
Call 1-800-873-8635 or visit www.ReaderService.com.

* Terms and prices subject to change without notice. Prices do not include applicable taxes. Sales tax applicable in N.Y. Canadian residents will be charged applicable taxes. Offer not valid in Quebec. This offer is limited to one order per household. Not valid for current subscribers to Harlequin Blaze books. All orders subject to credit approval. Credit or debit balances in a customer's account(s) may be offset by any other outstanding balance owed by or to the customer. Please allow 4 to 6 weeks for delivery. Offer available while quantities last.

Your Privacy—The Reader Service is committed to protecting your privacy. Our Privacy Policy is available online at www.ReaderService.com or upon request from the Reader Service.

We make a portion of our mailing list available to reputable third parties that offer products we believe may interest you. If you prefer that we not exchange your name with third parties, or if you wish to clarify or modify your communication preferences, please visit us at www.ReaderService.com/consumerschoice or write to us at Reader Service Preference Service, P.O. Box 9062, Buffalo, NY 14240-9062. Include your complete name and address.

HB15